WHAT DO PEOPLE SAY ABOUT THE OTHER BOOKS IN HUGH ASHTON'S SHERLOCK HOLMES SERIES?

THE DEED BOX OF JOHN H. WATSON M.D.

&

THE DISPATCH-BOX OF JOHN H. WATSON M.D.

"...Hugh Ashton maintains his place as one of the best writers of new Sherlock Holmes stories, in both plotting and style."
THE DISTRICT MESSENGER, NEWSLETTER OF THE
SHERLOCK HOLMES SOCIETY OF LONDON

"Hundreds of Holmes pastiches, ranging in quality from godawful to brilliant, are published every year. A few pastiche writers – ... Hugh Ashton, for example – sometimes are good enough to make you forget you're not reading the Master himself, having Watson narrate a lost but newly discovered story from some secret bank box or barrister's drawer."
DALLAS MORNING NEWS

"...delicately woven stories in the Conan Doyle tradition so that the reader cannot decipher where Conan Doyle's brilliant sleuth leaves off and where Ashton's begins. Truly a masterful addition to the Holmes legacy of wit, sleuthing and surprises!"
LINDA RAE BLAIR (AMAZON REVIEW)

Tales from the Deed Box of John H. Watson M.D.
Hugh Ashton

ISBN-13: 978-1-912605-03-3
ISBN-10: 1-912605-03-1
Published by j-views Publishing, 2018

www.j-views.biz

www.221BeanBakerStreet.info

j-views Publishing, 26 Lombard Street, Lichfield, UK, WS13 6DR

Tales From the
Deed Box
of
John H. Watson M.D.

DEDICATIONS

 ANY thanks to all who have helped in the production of these stories.

First, to my nephew Oliver Startin, whose Facebook posts prodded the Sherlock lurking in me into life;

To all my friends, in real life and on Facebook, who continue to inspire and encourage me;

To Arthur Conan Doyle, for his original creation of one of the most memorable friendships and one of the most extraordinary characters in English letters;

To the Beans at Inknbeans Press, especially the late "Boss Bean" Jo, whose good taste and good sense were instrumental in the production of these stories;

And last, but not least, to my wife Yoshiko, whose tolerance of my eccentricities and support of my efforts have encouraged me to go forward with this.

Contents

PREFACE TO THE 2012 EDITION

T was with great excitement that I first learned of a deed box that had been deposited in the vaults of one of our great London banks nearly one hundred years ago, and somehow left untouched and forgotten for most of that time. My friend at the bank told me that this box had stencilled on it in white paint the words "JOHN H. WATSON M.D. LATE INDIAN ARMY" on the top, with the initials "JHW" and the legend "TO BE LEFT UNTIL CALLED FOR" on the side.

Though Watson is a common name, and John even more so, any medical doctor of that era bearing that evocative name surely must recall an association with that most famous of detectives, Mr. Sherlock Holmes, who was at the height of his career in the decades immediately preceding the depositing of this box in the bank's vaults. The legal proceedings by which I eventually gained custody of the box are technical, and a very little interest to anyone except a lawyer (and it seems to me that even the most dedicated lawyer would find little of interest!).

On my opening of the box, I discovered a treasure trove – treasure, that is, for all who have followed the exploits of Sherlock Holmes and have been tantalised by the hints dropped by Watson concerning the cases about which he had written, but had never published. Two of these cases, *The Case of the Missing Matchbox* and *The Case of the Cormorant,* fall into this category. The hints dropped by Watson about these hitherto undescribed cases in his other accounts have long intrigued Holmes scholars.

When reading through the manuscripts in the deed box, it proved difficult to make a decision as to which tales to include and which to exclude. I have chosen here to include three tales which show hitherto unsuspected aspects of Holmes, some of which have been hinted at earlier by Watson.

One of the most interesting sidelights to be thrown on the career of Sherlock Holmes comes in the tale here entitled *The Odessa Business*. In this story we see a further side to Sherlock Holmes – that of his family. For a long time we have known about his reclusive and enigmatic brother, Mycroft. What was never alluded to by Watson in any of the published accounts was the existence of Evadne, his younger sister. She proves herself to be a true scion of the Holmes family, combining the energy of Sherlock with the raw mental capacity of his brother Mycroft. It is also refreshing to see familial affection between the siblings described in this story.

The second story here, the *Case of the Missing Matchbox*, deals with a bizarre crime, and also shows us a side of Sherlock Holmes which we might have guessed, or rather suspected, but which had remained unknown to us until this time. We have known from previous cases of his skill in fisticuffs, as well as in singlestick and the mysterious Japanese wrestling art of *baritsu* with which he bested Professor Moriarty in his battle above the Reichenbach Falls. Not until this time have we had a chance to discover the side of Holmes that delighted in single combat, and not for its own sake, but on behalf of those unable to defend themselves.

The final story in this short collection, the *Case of the Cormorant*, is to my knowledge unique in the canon of tales about Holmes. Watson alludes to this tale in another story, and it seems to have been regarded by him and probably by Holmes, as an "ace in the hole" to be played in the eventuality of an attack on Holmes or on Watson's records. It is, when one reads the story, not in the least unusual or strange that Watson should have withheld it from publication. The principal figure in the case, even had he been disguised by a pseudonym, would have been instantly recognisable to any contemporary, and it is quite likely that students of that period's history would likewise have encountered few difficulties of identification, even had the name and the location of the events described been changed. It is printed here in the hope that it will throw some light on some of the curious political machinations that occurred at this time.

I hope to spend more time deciphering the strange, almost illegible, doctor's writing that characterises these manuscripts, which cover many sheets of foolscap paper, now brittle with age, and requiring great care in their handling. I sincerely hope that the pleasure you obtain from reading these equals the pleasure I have had in reviving these figures from the past, who still live on in our minds as vividly as those personages we read about in our daily newspapers.

Hugh Ashton
Kamakura, 2012

PREFACE TO THE 2018 EDITION

 INCE writing the above, I have discovered many more Sherlock Holmes adventures which were published by Inknbeans Press, and been blessed with an enthusiastic group of readers who have been kind enough to let me know how much they have enjoyed my publications.

Thank you all so much for your support and enthusiasm.

In this period, I have also returned to the UK, moving from the historic city of Kamakura in Japan to the historic city of Lichfield in England. The change has been a big one, as you might imagine, and has been an inspiration in many ways.

However, there is a sad change to my circumstances – Inknbeans Press, who were the first publishers of these adventures, has now closed its doors, following the death of its founder and guiding spirit, Jo Lowe. She is mourned and missed, not just by me, but by all her authors, to whom she was much more than just an editor and publisher, but an inspiration and a friend.

Hugh Ashton
Lichfield, England, 2018

COLOPHON

E decided that this adventure of Sherlock Holmes deserved to be reproduced in paper form in as authentic a fashion as was possible given modern desktop publishing and print-on-demand technology.

Accordingly, after consulting the reproductions of the original Holmes adventures as printed in *The Strand Magazine*, we decided to use the Monotype Bruce Old Style font from Bitstream as the body (10.5 on 13.2). Though it would probably look better letterpressed than printed using a lithographic or laser method, and is missing old-style numerals, it still manages to convey the feel of the original.

The flowers are from the Bodini Ornaments font called, which have a little more of a 19th-century appearance than some of the alternatives.

Page headers are in Baskerville (what else can one use for a Holmes story?), and the titles are set in Amerante. The decorative drop caps are in Romantique, which preserves the feel of the Strand's original drop caps.

We have tried to carry out he punctuation according to the rules apparently followed by the *Strand*'s typesetters. These include double spacing after full stops (periods), spaces after opening quotation marks, and spaces on either side of punctuation such as question marks, exclamation marks and semi-colons. This seems to allow the type to breathe more easily, especially in long spoken and quoted exchanges, and we have therefore adopted this style here.

Some of the orthography has also been deliberately changed to match the original – for instance, " Baker Street" has become " Baker-street" throughout.

Tales From the Deed Box

of
John H. Watson M.D.

Three Untold Tales of
Sherlock Holmes

As Discovered By
Hugh Ashton

j-views Publishing, Lichfield, England

THE ODESSA BUSINESS

"I NOTICE THE BOTTLE IS SEALED, AND THE SEAL IS UNBROKEN.
MY GUESS IS THAT IT IS SOME SORT OF POISON." (PAGE 14)

EDITOR'S NOTE

This tale, which is not mentioned at all in any of the stories that Watson released to the world, came as a complete surprise to me when I first deciphered it from Watson's handwriting. Without a doubt, this is one of the more extraordinary revelations about the personal circumstances surrounding the great sleuth that I have so far encountered in the stories contained in the deed box. There may be more to come.

*We know little of Holmes' family life, other than the existence of brother Mycroft (*The Greek Interpreter *and* The Final Problem*). This story sheds an unexpected light on this aspect of the detective's existence, as well as showing him capable of hitherto unsuspected depths of family feeling.*

Y friend, the famous consulting detective Sherlock Holmes, was reticent about his family and his early life. Occasionally, indeed, as in his description of the affair of the *Gloria Scott*, he gave an account of his doings before he and I became acquainted, but my friend's family remained for the most part an enigma to me.

Nothing, it seemed, was of import to Holmes other than his pursuit of the solutions to the puzzles and mysteries that came to our door. It was one summer morning, when the metropolis seemed almost deserted, that I became aware of yet another side to the remorseless logician that had up to that time remained unsuspected by me.

For the previous two weeks, London had been what Holmes described as "plaguey dull", by which he signified that no major outbreak of criminal activity had occurred recently – a source of satisfaction to most law-abiding citizens, but a fount of frustration for Holmes, whose mind thrived on the crimes committed by the felons of the land and whose energies seemed replenished by the villainies of others. We were finishing an excellent breakfast, I remember, when the post was brought in by Mrs Hudson, our housekeeper, and deposited by Holmes' elbow, where it remained unopened as he devoted his attention to toast and marmalade.

At length he threw down his napkin and crossed to the large armchair, flinging himself into it.

"Ah, Watson," he remarked, "if only you could begin to guess at the ennui that afflicts me. Yesterday, I solved the mystery of the bisulphate of bismuth. My monograph on the regional differences in boot-nails, which should be of great service to the official police when they come to examine any footprints following the execution of a crime, is at the printer's, and I now have that Bach partita almost by heart. If you would be good enough to open the post, and provide me with a verbal *précis* of each item, I would be much obliged." So saying, he lounged back in his chair, and lit his foul-smelling pipe.

I picked up the first envelope.

"A ducal coronet," I observed. "This letter appears to be from His Grace the Duke of Shropshire."

"He will want to know about his son's losses at cards," replied Holmes, his eyes half-shut in that peculiar fashion of his, before I had even opened the envelope. "It is, of course, Colonel Sebastian Moran who has been cheating him, but the cunning devil has so many tricks and ruses that it would be almost impossible to prove it without my personally taking part in the game. And that, Watson, is something I am not prepared to do at this time."

"Astounding!" I exclaimed after having opened the envelope and read the contents. "You are absolutely correct in your guesses as to His Grace's wishes."

"Hardly guesses, Watson," he reproached me. "Put the letter on one side. We may decide to assist in this matter, if nothing more interesting or amusing comes to light." My friend's ideas of what events fell under those two headings were, I need hardly add, somewhat at odds with those possessed by the average Londoner. "I have long had my eye on Colonel Moran, and it would be a positive pleasure to remove him from the gaming rooms of the London clubs. Next letter, please."

I scanned the contents. "A Mrs Henrietta Cowling suspects her husband of a dalliance with an actress at the Criterion, and requests—"

"Next, Watson. I do not dabble in these petty affairs."

I picked up the next envelope, which gave off a faint scent that I was unable to place. I glanced at the back. "From St. Elizabeth's Academy for Young Ladies, Brighton," I remarked.

"Read it," commanded Holmes. He had not altered his position as he lounged in the chair, but to someone who knew him as intimately as myself, there was a subtle change in his attitude. "Extraordinary!" I burst out, when I had finished perusing the epistle. "The lady who wrote this has the same surname as yourself. Miss Evadne Holmes."

"Indeed?" replied my friend. A strange sort of half-smile, almost unnoticeable, played about his lips. "Perhaps you would be good enough to inform me of its contents after ascertaining some more information about this establishment?" He waved a lazy hand towards the shelves of reference works.

I reached for the Almanac, and proceeded to ascertain the facts regarding St. Elizabeth's.

"Of course." I summarized the contents of the entry I had just read. "The lady is the principal of this academic institution, where nearly one hundred young ladies are educated, founded by her to provide young ladies with a sound general education on Christian principles, in the year—"

"Enough, Watson. Proceed with the letter."

I turned to the sheets of stiff paper that comprised the epistle. "Among the pupils there is the young Russian Archduchess Anastasia, who is completing her studies in this country. A few nights ago, three to be precise, the young lady was disturbed by a noise at the window of the room shared with ten other girls, and she saw what she described as a hideous bearded face peering through a gap in the curtains. She was, not unnaturally, frightened by this, as were the other girls in the room, and the alarm was raised, but a search by the principal and the mistresses of the academy discovered no trace of the intruder."

"No trace?" remarked Holmes. "I had thought better of Evadne."

I looked at him sharply, but he gave no clue as to the meaning of that utterance. "She requests your help in investigating this matter," I concluded. "Shall I put this on one side with the Duke of Shropshire's epistle, or consign it to the rubbish with Mrs Cowling's?"

"Neither, Watson. I believe that the sea air at Brighton will do us both good. Let us start this morning. But before we set off, what do you learn from this letter?"

"Little, I fear. There is a strange smell about the paper that I cannot, for the life of me, place. It is written in violet ink – unusual, but not so unusual. There is little I can deduce from this."

"The smell, I would guess, is carbolic soap."

I put the envelope once more to my nostrils and inhaled. "Indeed it is, Holmes!" The smell was now familiar to me. "How—?"

"I doubt if Evadne's habits have changed with middle age," he remarked, somewhat enigmatically. "My dear fellow, you have missed many of the important points. The writer is left-handed, no?" I used what little skill in graphology I had acquired to examine the letter, and was forced to agree with Holmes' guess, if that is what it was. "But I think you have missed the most significant point of this letter." His smile was now plain to see. "What is the superscription?"

I examined the letter once again. " 'My dear Sherlock',"

I read. "This seems a most intimate form of address for a client to use. The lady is a relation of yours?"

"My sister," he replied, enjoying my obvious surprise.

I had met Holmes' brother Mycroft once, in the matter of the Greek interpreter, but Holmes had never alluded to any other brothers or sisters.

"She is, without a doubt, the intellectual equal of my brother Mycroft, and, but for the accident of her sex, would no doubt occupy the same place in government he currently holds. As it is, she advises the Treasury on matters of finance and the Foreign Office on diplomacy under a male pseudonym through Mycroft while maintaining St. Elizabeth's Academy to occupy her idle moments. She is also, as you may or may not be aware, a contributor to various mathematical journals, again using a male alias. She recently achieved something in the nature of an academic triumph over Professor James Moriarty, in her rebuttal of his treatise upon the binomial theorem. I must confess, however, that Evadne and I have not seen each other for a number of years, not on account of any animosity between us – indeed, as children we were remarkably close, and that attachment has never entirely disappeared – but simply through indolence, chiefly on my part, I fear. It is time for me to strengthen the family bonds again, Watson, and, as I mentioned, the change of air will do us good, trapped as we are in the metropolis. Be so good as to look up a convenient time in Bradshaw."

Before I could fulfil this request, there was a knock at our door, and Mrs Hudson announced the arrival of Inspector Lestrade of Scotland Yard. The small man almost bounded into the room in a state of excitement.

"Halloa!" exclaimed Holmes. "What brings you here straight from your home? Help yourself to coffee, and sit yourself down in that chair. But how did your small change come to rest in the right-hand pocket of your trousers? Do you not find it inconvenient to have Mrs Lestrade arrange the contents of your pockets of a morning?"

Lestrade looked from Holmes to me and shrugged. "Another of your conjuring tricks, Mr Holmes?"

"Hardly, my dear Inspector. I have had occasion previously to notice that you are left-handed, and the present mild disarray of your garments indicates to me that you have reached across to extract something from the right-hand pocket, thereby disarranging your clothes. The object would hardly be your watch, that I see is placed in a place convenient for your left hand, and I scarcely imagine that you would need your keys when you have come to pay us a visit. I therefore deduce that you found it necessary to reach into that pocket to extract some money for the purpose of paying the fare of the hansom I heard draw up a few minutes ago."

"And how did you know that I had come straight from my home?"

"Tut, man. I cannot imagine Inspector Lestrade entering the hallowed precincts of Scotland Yard with flecks of shaving soap behind one ear, and one boot improperly laced. But when you are visiting the humble abode of Sherlock Holmes, such matters are presumably of no importance..."

Lestrade laughed ruefully. "You are too much for me," he confessed. "But I admit that your assistance would be most useful in a case that was brought to my attention by a telegram brought to my house this morning, followed by a longer dispatch from the Yard."

As he spoke there was another knock on the door, and Mrs Hudson presented a telegram to Holmes.

"Ha!" he ejaculated, ripping open the envelope, and scribbling a few words on the reply form. "Take this to the post-office, if you would, Mrs Hudson. You were saying, Inspector?" as Mrs Hudson left the room.

"Yes, Mr Holmes. I would greatly value your knowledge of European matters in helping me with this affair. It concerns an educational establishment for young ladies in Brighton—"

"St Elizabeth's, I believe?" smiled Holmes.

Lestrade gave a visible start in his seat. "How the deuce do you know that?" he said.

Holmes smiled. "I believe we have both received communications this morning referring to the same incident. Maybe you have a little more information from the report to which you alluded than do I at this present time? Perhaps we could travel to Brighton together, and you could occupy the time by recounting the facts as you know them? Oh, and if you wish to remove that shaving soap to which I alluded previously, feel free to avail yourself of this establishment's ablutionary facilities."

 E arrived at Brighton at about midday. Lestrade had informed us of the events at St Elizabeth's as we sat in our first-class carriage. It seemed that the mysterious bearded visitor mentioned in Miss Holmes' letter had been seen again at ten o'clock the previous evening, again by the young Archduchess, in the same way as before, peering through the curtains. Again the alarm had been raised, and a search party sent out, aided this time by several of the male teaching staff and the gardener, who had been requested to stay on the premises that evening by Miss Holmes, contrary to usual custom.

This time, the search had not been fruitless. A body whose countenance, as far as could be ascertained, resembled that seen by the girls earlier in the evening had been found by the French master, Monsieur Leboeuf, lying in a flowerbed, on the opposite side of the building to the window where the face had been observed. Firmly implanted in the chest of the dead man, and seemingly the cause of his death, was a long paperknife, subsequently identified as the property of the principal herself.

"Intriguing," Holmes had remarked, listening to Lestrade's narrative, his eyes closed, and his fingers steepled in that characteristic pose of his. "And what does the owner of the knife have to say about this?"

"Miss Holmes," replied Lestrade, "insists that although the knife is hers, it had disappeared from the desk in her study some two or three days before – she cannot be exactly certain – and that she had no idea where it was until it reappeared as the apparent murder weapon. By the by, it is curious, Mr Holmes, that you and she should share the same name."

"I believe it is common," replied Holmes sardonically, "for a brother and sister to share a name."

Lestrade stared at Holmes in astonishment, and the notebook from which he had been reading dropped from his hand. "I had no idea..." he stammered. "You have a personal interest in this case, then?"

"You requested my assistance on this case," replied Holmes coldly. "I shall give it to the best of my ability, regardless of any family ties that may be present."

"Just so, just so," muttered Lestrade, obviously embarrassed.

I was anxious to restore some semblance of social ease to the gathering. "Perhaps you can tell us what is known about the murdered man?" I suggested to Lestrade.

The police inspector retrieved his notebook and started reading from it, with an obvious sense of relief at being delivered from his gaffe. "From papers found on him, the dead man appears to have been a Russian, by the name of Plekhoff. His passport shows he entered England a week ago. As of this morning, the Sussex police have been unable to discover where he has been staying."

"Of course, there is no reason for them to assume that he was staying locally," remarked Holmes. "The train service to London from Brighton is a particularly good one, and the last trains leave a little before midnight, I believe."

"True, true," agreed Lestrade.

"Have any arrests been made?" asked Holmes.

"If you are concerned for your sister," replied Lestrade, with an obvious attempt at reconciliation, "I am happy to tell you that the Sussex police saw no grounds for her arrest simply as a result of the murder weapon having belonged to her."

"Thank you," replied Holmes, and gazed out of the window. Without turning his head, he addressed us both. "May I trouble you both to remain silent until we reach Brighton? I wish to consider this matter." So saying, he pulled out his pipe and proceeded to almost asphyxiate both of us until we arrived at the Brighton London Road station, and were able to pull fresh air into our suffering lungs.

E were greeted by Inspector Steere of the Sussex Constabulary, a ruddy-faced guardian of the law of the old school.

"Well pleased to have you with us," he said to Lestrade. "These foreign doings to do with Russia are somewhat out of our league, and we welcome help from London on these matters."

"You suspect that the Russians are involved, then?" asked Holmes.

Steere looked inquiringly at Holmes, and Lestrade hastened to introduce us.

"Well, I've heard of you, Mr. Holmes, and you too, Dr. Watson, and I am well pleased to see both of you here, too. In answer to your question, it stands to reason, doesn't it, that it's all connected with the Rooskies? That young Archduchess and all that?"

"Quite so," replied Holmes, though I knew from his expression that his words belied his true feelings on the matter. "May we visit the scene of the crime?"

"The cab's waiting, sir. The body is just where it was

found."

When we arrived at St. Elizabeth's, a handsome red-brick mansion, I was somewhat surprised that Holmes made no immediate attempt to meet his sister, but allowed himself to be led immediately to the scene where the body had been discovered and still lay, covered by a tarpaulin cloth, that was withdrawn by two constables as we approached.

The dead man appeared to have been somewhat short of stature, slightly built. His most distinguishing feature was the heavy beard that surrounded his face. Holmes dropped to one knee, and whipped out his powerful magnifying lens, peering through it at the body, as well as at the hilt of the ornamental paperknife that protruded from the cadaver's chest, surrounded by a small brown stain on the man's shirtfront, presumably dried blood.

"An interesting weapon," I remarked, looking at the curiously wrought Oriental workmanship.

"Turkish, according to Miss Holmes," replied Steere.

"She has positively identified it as hers?" asked Lestrade.

"As positive as anyone could be under the circumstances, sir. We have no formal statement from her as yet."

Holmes appeared to have finished his inspection of the corpse, and was now examining the ground around it. "Has the body been moved?" he asked.

"No, sir," replied Steere. "We were at great pains to leave everything as it was found ready for the gentlemen from London. The only thing we did was to empty his pockets."

"So I observe from the mess you fellows made with your footprints," Holmes remarked a little testily. "I shall want to see what you found later on. Very good," he added, standing up, "I've seen enough here. Let us now examine the window where this man allegedly showed his face."

"'Allegedly', sir? Surely there is no doubt. Her Highness and several of the other girls have testified already to having seen him looking through the window."

"As you will, Inspector. Of what room is this the window,

by the way?"

"This is the principal's study, sir," replied the Sussex inspector.

We marched round to the back of the building, where a constable was standing. "We thought it best to take no chances," said Steere. "There might be something to be learned here, we felt."

"Quite right, Inspector," replied Holmes. "This may make up for your men's blundering around near the body." Once more he dropped to the ground, this time lying full length on the damp soil, heedless of his garments, as he peered at the marks in the flower-bed.

"Ha! As I thought," he remarked at length, arising from his recumbent position, and stretching himself to peer through the window. He picked something that appeared to be some kind of dark tangled thread from the creeper that covered the wall beside the window, placing it in an envelope with an expression of satisfaction

"You never change, do you, Sherlock?" came a cultivated feminine voice from behind us. "Always dirtying your clothes, peeking at things that don't belong to you, and keeping your secrets to yourself."

I turned to face the speaker. The family resemblance was obvious at a glance. Miss Evadne Holmes was a true feminine counterpart of her brother, with the same aquiline nose, deep-set eyes and thin compressed lips. Her strong face would have been somewhat unattractive in a woman, had it not been tempered by a flash of obvious humour that was often lacking in her brother's countenance.

"Evadne!" he exclaimed. The pleasure at meeting his sister seemed unfeigned, and showed a facet of his character hitherto unseen by me. "Excuse me," he apologised to her. "A little of your flower-bed appears to have adhered to my hands. May I clean myself up a little? And then, Inspector, if we may examine the contents of the dead man's pockets?"

Holmes allowed himself to be led by his sister, presumably

to some hot water and towels, for he emerged some minutes later looking somewhat less like a rural ploughman.

"Yes, indeed, Russian, as you say," he remarked, examining the papers headed by the Romanoff double eagle. "And, as I thought, Lestrade." He held up a scrap of pasteboard. "Here we have the return half of a railway ticket from Victoria Station dated yesterday. He was intending to return last night. It would be singularly useless to begin looking for his lodgings in this area late at night. And this here," sniffing at a small packet. "Yes, Russian tobacco, I have no doubt. Wouldn't you agree, Lestrade?" holding out the paper for the other's inspection.

"I would have no idea about that," replied the policeman. "I have little experience of these things."

"I would lay pennies to a pound I am correct," my friend answered. "A small penknife, of cheap German manufacture, and this bottle. What does it contain, Inspector?"

"We have had no time to submit it to analysis, sir," pointed out Steere, somewhat nettled.

"Just so, just so," replied Holmes, conciliatory. "I notice the bottle is sealed, and the seal is unbroken. My guess is that it is some sort of poison."

"We'd observed the unbroken seal, too, sir, and truth to tell, I'd made the same guess as yourself."

"And that appears to be all, doesn't it? Other than this piece of cardboard printed in Russian, which I cannot read. Our late friend travelled light, it would appear. I would like to speak with the Archduchess in the presence of one of the academic staff, if I may."

"I'm sure that can be arranged, Mr Holmes," replied Lestrade. "If I may, sir, under the circumstances, I feel it would be wisest if the member of staff were someone other than your sister?"

"Naturally," replied Holmes, easily. "I would have suggested the same thing myself if you had not mentioned it."

BOUT ten minutes later, the two police inspectors, Holmes, and myself were seated in a small room together with Miss Simpson, who had been introduced to us as the senior history mistress.

"I trust that you will say or do nothing that will alarm the poor child further," she requested, showing a degree of compassion for her charges that was at odds with her stern forbidding appearance.

"I will endeavour to exercise all the tact and restraint of which I am capable," replied Holmes, with the easy good humour for which he was famous.

The girl was shown in, and we all rose. Truly, I think I have hardly ever seen a more beautiful and nobly self-possessed young woman than the Archduchess Anastasia. She was dressed in the drab grey uniform of the school, but she entered as though she had been decked in a ball gown and a diamond tiara. There was something regal in the way she sat, and faced us with a level gaze with calm grey eyes from within a halo of golden hair.

"Your Highness," Holmes began. "I have a few simple questions to ask you, and though I am not of the police and you are therefore under no obligation to answer my questions, it would be in the interests of justice if you would do me the favour of indulging my curiosity." She bowed her graceful head in assent. "Can you tell us the exact time at which you saw the man at the window?"

"You mean on the second occasion? Last night?" Her English had only the faintest trace of a foreign accent. Holmes nodded. "Yes. It was exactly ten o'clock. The stable clock had just begun striking ten, and that is the time when we are required to put out our lights. I was just moving to snuff out my candle when I saw the face at the window."

"Did you recognise the man?"

"Of course not!"

"I am sorry. That was not my meaning. What I meant

to ask you was whether the man you saw last night was the same as the man whom you saw previously looking through your window."

"I am sure of it. The same bearded face appeared on both occasions. How can you doubt my word on it?"

"I am not doubting your word, Your Highness. I simply wished to be certain of the matter. I have only one more question for you at present, which may be difficult for you to answer, but I must ask it. Are you aware if you, or any of your family, are the target of any anarchist or nihilist threats?"

A slight tremor filled her voice as she replied. "Yes, indeed. My father has been the subject of at least two attempts on his life, and it has been feared by the Russian authorities that my sisters and I may also be the target of the anarchists. I am not frightened of them, though." These were brave words, but they failed to carry conviction to my ears, at least. Holmes, on the other hand, seemed satisfied.

"Thank you, Your Highness. That will be all for the present."

She rose, and we all rose with her as she left the room, escorted by the formidable Miss Simpson.

"I think we have it now, Mr Holmes, thanks to you," said Lestrade, "though I have no doubt we would have reached the same conclusion without your help."

"Indeed?" Holmes cocked a sardonic eye. "And pray, what conclusion have you reached?"

"The dead man was one of these Russian nihilist anarchists that you mentioned just now. He arrived here with the intent of killing the girl, or maybe abducting her. The phial in his pockets no doubt contains poison, as we agreed, or maybe some sort of sleeping draught which he proposed to administer if abduction was his goal. The first night he made his appearance, he realised that he had been seen, and accordingly made his escape. He returned a few nights later, and was seen again, but this time, the hue and cry was more successful than on the previous occasion. He was discovered by your sister, who surprised him as he was creeping away in his attempt to escape. She bravely attacked him with the paperknife, which she had snatched up as she went outside, and he died in the struggle. Naturally, she wishes to deny any such thing, as she is frightened she will be accused of murder. Well, I would like you to tell her, Mr Holmes, that in this case, we won't be pressing charges. I can give you my word on that. The death of one of that type is no great loss, I can assure you."

"You would indeed be foolish to press charges," replied Holmes. "I fear you are on completely the wrong scent. It is a beautiful story, Lestrade. It lacks only the virtue of truth."

Lestrade snorted. "And which of your precious theories is it to be this time, Mr Holmes? Surely the answer is staring you in the face."

"Some of the answers were staring us in the face, it is true. But other questions remain. I think we need to speak to Monsieur Leboeuf now."

Inspector Steere passed a request to a constable, who left, returning a few minutes later shaking his head. "Beg pardon, sir," he said to Steere, "but they can't find the gentleman anywhere. Seems no-one's set eyes on him since last night when he found the body."

"Confound you!" said Holmes angrily to the Sussex policeman. "You've let him slip through your fingers."

I noticed that Lestrade seemed a little less cocksure than he had done a few minutes previously. "I am sure that Inspector Steere has done his best," he said.

"I think it is time I talked to my sister," said Holmes. "In private, if you have no objection, gentlemen. Watson, I require you as a witness. Come." He stalked off, and I followed.

E entered Miss Holmes' study, where she received us pleasantly enough, and greeted me by name.

"I have always enjoyed reading your accounts of Sherlock's adventures," she told me. "I must admit that I never thought I would feature as a character in one of them."

"Well, Evadne," said her brother, settling himself into a chair opposite the desk. "There is more to this than the police know and you want to tell them, is there not? Does Mycroft know what has happened here?"

"No, he does not, and I do not wish him to be informed by you, Sherlock, or by anyone else. He suffers from a weak heart, as you know, and the shock would be bad for him. The country can hardly afford to lose him at this hour." I pondered briefly on the workings of this strange family, who seemed to hold the fate of the nation in their hands, before my attention returned to their conversation. "It concerns the Russian treaty."

"Ah," said Holmes. "The Odessa business?" This was completely outside my sphere of knowledge, and I had no conception of what was being discussed.

Miss Holmes nodded. "The very same. I do not know if Mycroft informed you of the details?"

"The vaguest outlines only."

"I will not bore you with the minutiae, but suffice it to say that if the French government were to learn of what had been agreed..." She shrugged her shoulders and spread her hands in what I took to be a comic parody of a typical Gallic gesture. "The final draft was here in this room."

"Was?" interjected her brother. "And it vanished at the same time as your paperknife?"

She sighed. "Why do I bother telling my brothers anything? They are always telling me that they know it all before I open my mouth," she complained to me, humorously. "No, you cannot be right all the time, Sherlock," returning to seriousness. "It vanished last night. The paperknife vanished two days ago."

"The day after our mysterious Russian was first seen peering in at the window, in fact?"

"I suppose so. Yes, that is correct."

"And soon after you had had occasion to converse with Monsieur Leboeuf in this room? Monsieur Leboeuf is a tall man, I take it? About as tall as me? And clean-shaven, of course."

"Of course he is, Sherlock. Why do you bother confirming the obvious after your exertions in the flowerbeds outside? But it was not after I had talked with him that the knife vanished, it was after I had been holding a discussion in this room with the drawing master, Monsieur Delasse."

Sherlock Holmes' eyes positively sparkled. "Better and better!" he exclaimed. "We have it all now, I think. Watson, you and I will have a word or two with Monsieur Delasse. How long has he been with you, Evadne?"

"Since the start of this term only," she replied.

"And how long was Monsieur Leboeuf in your employ? I use the past tense, because I fear you will never see him again. He is now," looking at his watch, "probably stepping off the ferry from Newhaven in Dieppe."

"Two terms. I now see what you mean, Sherlock. Since the Odessa business. What a fool I have been."

"Hardly, Evadne. I am sure they came with excellent references and were both skilled teachers. You cannot allow yourself to take any blame."

She smiled. "Indeed they were excellent instructors. I will say that much for them. It will be difficult to replace them with others of equal competence." There was a somewhat ironic smile on her face, which reminded me of her brother's occasional moods. Her ability to see such a side to even the worst of prospects made me warm to her.

"Never fear. I am sure something can be arranged for you and your pupils. Where will we find Monsieur Delasse?"

She told us. "Come, Watson."

The drawing master's room was what might be expected of a Frenchman of an artistic persuasion. Pictures of a certain indelicacy hung on the walls, and certain smells that were not of English provenance filled the air. The man himself was a very caricature of a certain type of Frenchman, with waxed upturned moustaches, and a nervous excitable manner.

"But what is it you want?" he positively squeaked at us.

"I merely heard of your collection of interesting drawings," remarked Holmes, "and I wondered if you would grant us the pleasure of admiring them."

"I heard you were of the police," said Delasse.

"With them, but not of them," replied Holmes. "The distinction will become clear if you are to cooperate with us by showing us your most interesting drawings."

The other shrugged, and I saw the source of Miss Holmes' comical imitation. "If that is what you wish, *messieurs*."

He fetched a portfolio of papers, and spread them out on the table. "This one here, by Renoir. Observe the fineness and delicacy of the lines."

No matter how fine or delicate the lines might have been, the subject matter was less than delicate, and showed our Gallic cousins' lack of restraint in matters of the heart. Holmes appeared to be unconcerned with the subject of the drawings, however, and waved his hands over the paper.

"No, no. I mean your latest acquisitions. The ones you came by last night."

"What are you talking about?" His eyes showed his fear, darting from one of us to the other.

Holmes sighed. "I was hoping that you would display the aptitude for logic for which Frenchmen are famous. But since that is not to be..." He turned as if to leave the room, and put a small whistle to his lips, but did not blow it.

"Wait! I can help you, I think." He hurriedly reached

for another portfolio, and extracted a sheaf of handwritten foolscap sheets.

"Thank you," said Holmes, receiving the proffered papers, and tucking them in an inside pocket after glancing through them. "And now, if you tell us the truth, there is a very good chance that you may follow your colleague home on the next boat from Newhaven."

"And if I refuse?"

"Then there is every certainty that I will call the police and have you arrested."

"I never killed him!" wailed the Frenchman. "That was of Jacques' doing, I swear before God."

"Throttled, I take it? But then you and he dragged the body together to Miss Holmes' window and it was you who rifled her study while Monsieur Leboeuf put on his false beard and looked through the girl's window to frighten her. I must give you credit for allowing Leboeuf to 'discover' the body. Who would ever suspect the man who discovered the body to be the very man who committed the murder? Whose idea was it to use the Russian as a decoy?"

"Jacques'. Originally, our plan was simply to steal the papers, taking some plate and other valuables to make it appear as a burglary. You understand, *hein*? But this anarchist appearing was a gift from God. The girl, Anastasia, gave no description of the man except that of a great bushy beard, which she sketched at my request. It was easy to procure a facsimile. Jacques, being taller, was the one to wear it and look in at the window to distract attention from my work at the other side of the building. I had already marked the place where the papers were kept. We waited, he and I, for the Russian to appear—"

"How did you know he would appear that night?" interjected Holmes.

"We did not. We were prepared to wait every night for a week or longer if needed. In the event, we had only to wait a few nights. He entered through the back entrance of the grounds. We sprang on him, and I held him, while Jacques did his work. He struggled a little, and then – *pouf* ! "

" And the dagger? "

" I had taken it from the study after my interview with Miss Holmes. I had a feeling that it would be useful in the future."

" The artistic feeling," Holmes sneered. " Why did you not take these," he tapped his pocket, " at the same time? "

The other gave another of his comic shrugs. "*Alors*, how could I do that? They were in front of her face, in plain view. The knife, that was different. That I could take without notice."

" And why," I asked, " are the papers still here? Why are they not with Leboeuf in Dieppe? "

Holmes shot me a glance, I am proud to say, that seemed to bespeak admiration.

" Because, *monsieur*, there was every chance that he would be stopped by the police. You have missed him by a matter of hours only. Who would think of looking for these papers here, when the bird has flown from the nest? "

" Indeed," chuckled Holmes. " One last question. How did you discover that the papers were here and the true nature of my sister's work? "

" Your sister? You are Sherlock Holmes? " Holmes nodded, and the other grinned, unexpectedly. " No wonder we were discovered. The famous Sherlock Holmes. We had no chance, did we? But to answer your question, which is a good one, I can swear to you before God, on my mother's grave, in any form you please, that neither Jacques nor I have any knowledge of this through our own efforts. The orders came from the Quai d'Orsay to come here and do this work. Other than that, I cannot help you. Believe me."

" I believe you," said Holmes simply. " You are free to go. I would advise going now, and not bother packing any of your belongings."

The little man looked stunned. " You mean it? "

"I gave you my word. Now go."

We turned and went down the stairs, returning to Miss Holmes' room.

As we descended, I could not refrain from asking Holmes why he had allowed a man who was not only an accomplice to murder, but also an enemy of our country, to go free.

"The dead man is no great loss to the world," replied Holmes. "Even Lestrade has the good sense to recognise this fact. As to the other, it is better for all concerned if the matter is kept hidden, and is not exposed to public view, which, in the event of a criminal trial, would undoubtedly be the case. It may be that I am not strictly within the bounds of the law here, but I am certain that I am in the right. I am confident that I can persuade Lestrade, through hints, of the justice of my actions, and my conscience is clear on the matter."

We knocked on the study door, and were bidden to enter.

"We discovered this in Monsieur Delasse's room," said Holmes, handing over to his sister a sheaf of drawings, which I had observed him pick up as we left the drawing master.

Miss Holmes glanced through them, and her cheeks flushed. "Sherlock, you cannot shock me so easily. I may not be a married woman, but I know the ways of the world. This is a bad joke on your part." She raised her hand as if to strike him, but Holmes stepped back.

"Forgive my antic sense of humour, Evadne. Maybe the next page will be more to your liking." She turned the page and came across the foolscap writing. Her eyes lit up, and her hand, which had been raised to slap my friend across the face, was joined by its partner in an embrace around his neck.

"You dear darling Sherlock!" she exclaimed. "You have saved me!"

"And Mycroft, and my own reputation, come to that," said Holmes, who was as close to total embarrassment as I have ever beheld him. I turned away to spare his feelings.

"Of course."

"Now I must go and put Lestrade's mind at rest," said Holmes, "before he starts to go off on one of his flights of fancy and arrests the gardener. A good fellow in his tenacity – like a bulldog, in fact – but sadly lacking in imagination, except when it comes to deciding who is guilty of a crime. I think I can persuade him that Leboeuf is the guilty party – which he is, by the way – and that it would be a waste of Lestrade's time to pursue the matter any further. The fact that Leboeuf has flown the coop should be enough to persuade him of that."

"But you and Dr. Watson will stay to dinner, I hope, before you return to London?"

"I gratefully accept, on behalf of Sherlock and myself," I replied, wishing to learn more of this intriguing lady, who was at the same time so similar to, but yet so different from my friend. Holmes looked at me reproachfully and shook his head, but said nothing.

T was obvious to me from the first sight of the body, Watson," said Holmes, as we sat in our rooms in Baker-street. "Surely you, as a medical man, must have noticed the blatant incongruity. A live man stabbed through the heart would surely lose more blood than the trickle we discovered beside the body and staining his clothes."

"I remarked the fact at the time," I replied, "but could not attach any great significance to it."

"But," continued Holmes, "you must know that a cadaver stabbed in the same way loses much less blood – about the same amount, in fact, as we discovered."

"You mean he was dead when the knife was plunged into his heart?"

"Pah! That simple fact was obvious from so many clues.

Did you not observe his boots? They were completely free of any mud and, as you undoubtedly noticed, the ground was soft and heavy. Not only that, but there were obvious signs that the body had been dragged to its resting place from somewhere else. Those ignoramuses of the local police had obscured almost all other footprints, but that much, at the least, was clear."

" But why did they leave the body outside your sister's study? Surely that would draw attention to the fact that the papers had been stolen?"

" Hardly that, Watson. Consider. There was an intruder. His body is discovered. The missing papers, should my sister ever have announced the fact of their having being stolen, were not on his body. This was a blind, Watson, a blind to lead Lestrade and the rest of them in the wrong direction. Who would ever suspect there was a thief on the premises, if the suspected thief's body was there, paperless?"

" And why not leave the body outside the girl's room?"

" Come, Watson, surely you can answer that one for yourself? Did you not notice the height of the window? How I had to stretch myself on the tips of my toes to peer through it? And I am not a small man."

" And the dead man was indeed a small man!" I exclaimed, with a flash of insight.

" Bravo, Watson! Even the Sussex police would have come to that conclusion eventually. Furthermore, I noticed the footprints in the flowerbed that were almost identical in shape to the ones I left after I had strained to peer through the window. From which, I naturally deduced that the man outside the window was about my height. You saw me retrieve a tuft of fibre from the false beard, which had evidently caught on the plant creeping up the wall. Added to which, the soil took an excellent impression, and the marks of the boots showed clear indications of their being of French manufacture. The missing Monsieur Leboeuf was obviously the man who had frightened our little Russian

Archduchess so badly on the second occasion. However, there were also marks, though not so distinct, of some sort of box or platform having been placed there in the past few days. We can assume that the Russian had used some sort of seed-box or packing crate as a support the other day when he was spotted through the window."

"And the other?"

"There were faint traces, though the police had done their best to erase them, of another pair of boots near the body. These were of French manufacture. I guessed it quite likely that there would be a drawing master, or music instructor of some kind on the staff, and so it transpired. When my sister had explained the existence of the draft of the treaty, the rest was obvious, once you understand the workings of the French mind. It would have been easy for the French authorities to insert the agents into the school, and for them to discover my sister's habits with regard to her government work. We may assume that Leboeuf and Delasse are among the foremost practitioners of their kind. Their methods were almost cruder versions of those that I would employ myself, should I ever find myself engaged in such an enterprise."

"It seems so simple when you explain it."

"Quite so," he replied shortly. "Now, I suppose, I may return to that Bach partita. Maybe you would be good enough, Watson, to draft on my behalf a reply to the Duke of Shropshire advising him to order his son to keep a safe distance from Colonel Moran."

THE CASE OF THE MISSING MATCHBOX

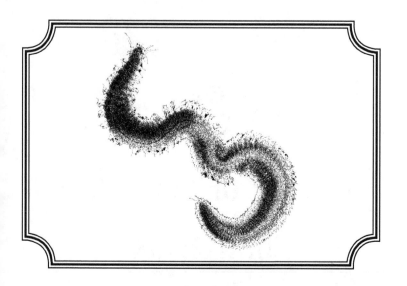

"…THE HIDEOUS PINK FLESHY HEAD OF SOME VILE WORM-
LIKE CREATURE EMERGED. SOME KIND OF GREEN LIQUID
DROOLED FROM WHAT I TOOK TO BE ITS JAWS." (PAGE 50)

EDITOR'S NOTE

In the account of the case entitled Thor Bridge, *Dr. Watson alludes to "A third case worthy of note … that of Isadora Persano, the well-known journalist and duellist, who was found stark staring mad with a match box in front of him which contained a remarkable worm said to be unknown to science," categorizing this as a "failure, since no final explanation is forthcoming". It is feared that the good doctor's memory was at fault here, since this case, which for some reason remained unpublished by him, possibly in an attempt to protect the name of one of the principals in the case (although Watson used a pseudonym here) was indeed solved by Holmes, at least to the detective's satisfaction. It is here presented to the public for the first time, the line of the unfortunate "Professor Schinkenbein" having died out, meaning that no scandal can now be associated with the late maestro.*

T is one of the pities of our age," my friend Sherlock Holmes remarked to me one day, "that duelling is no longer in fashion."

"On the contrary," I retorted, "I count it as one of the blessings of our civilised world that a man need no longer fear being shot dead or run through with a sword on account of a few careless words he may have uttered. Why do you say otherwise ? "

"I was merely considering the affair of Isadora Persano, as reported in today's *Morning Post*."

"You speak of the opera critic ? "

"The same. It seems that last night while he was dining at his favourite restaurant in Piccadilly, he came into conflict with the composer of operas and other works that have been the subject of recent adverse criticism by Persano for some time now. The composer approached him, and slapped his face with a glove. Persano's Latin blood rose to the insult, and the result was a challenge along the classic lines of a meeting at dawn on Hampstead Heath. Naturally, the other diners in the restaurant overheard the heated exchange, and the police were called, with the result that both men are now in custody."

"And why do you consider it so regrettable that the composer was not permitted to obtain the satisfaction that he imagined he deserved ? "

"Because I attended one of the performances criticised by Persano, and though I generally find myself in agreement with his judgements, in this case I consider his opinion to be sadly mistaken. The work in question was, to my mind, one of the finest musical productions to be encountered in many a year. The worlds of both journalism and music would have been well served, Watson, if Persano had been exposed to the displeasure of Herr Professor Schinkenbein. I very much doubt if the result would have been fatal on either side, despite Persano's reputation in these matters, but a salutary lesson might have been imparted."

I should add here that the world-famous personage I allude to in these pages as "Professor Schinkenbein" bore a different name in reality. To spare his surviving family further embarrassment, I have employed this pseudonym throughout.

Holmes spoke light-heartedly, but yet with some asperity. I happened to know that his work on a recent case had been the subject of some controversy in the columns of the *Morning Post*, where he had drawn the fire of a writer who seemed determined to denigrate his efforts, and I was therefore unsurprised to hear him speak this way of the press.

"Come, Holmes," I expostulated. "Duelling is the practice of an older and more barbaric age, and it is well that we of this country have outgrown the practice. Persano, whatever his origins—"

"Argentinian," interjected Holmes.

"—should learn that we are a civilised country and do

not tolerate such practices here."

Holmes cocked a quizzical eye at me. "Then it would surprise you to learn that I have had at least seven such meetings in the past three years ? "

I started from my seat. "Holmes ! " I exclaimed. "I had no idea of these activities of yours. On what grounds have you been engaged in these *affaires d'honneur* ? You must promise me that this practice must cease. Obviously, since you are here and we are conversing together, you must have come out as the victor on these occasions. I hardly like to ask, but..."

"What happened to my opponents ? " Holmes finished my thoughts. "I am happy to say that they still walk the streets of this fair city, chastened, and sadder, but yet wiser men. I have yet to make a permanent disposition of any of them, but it will be a long time, if ever, before they repeat the follies that led them to meet me under those circumstances."

"These were not personal insults that led you to this course, then ? "

"By no means, Watson. Though I am not without my share of self-regard," (I smiled inwardly to myself at this, for if Sherlock Holmes suffered from a fault, it was one of excessive pride in his admittedly considerable abilities) "I do not regard insults against my person as being worthy of the death of the utterer of the same. These conflicts were, if you will, an attempt to force a course of self-reflection on those individuals who prey on and abuse those who are weaker than themselves, and possess no means of self-defence."

I was pondering the singular morality of this position, when we heard a ring at the front door.

"A client ? " I asked Holmes.

"I am not expecting any such," replied Holmes. In a few minutes, however, there was a knock at the door of our rooms, and Mrs. Hudson ushered in a heavily built elderly gentleman, with a shock of white hair atop a round, somewhat cherubic face. When he removed his hat and overcoat, he revealed, despite the earliness of the hour, formal evening wear, albeit in some disarray. A scarlet cravat at his throat, secured with a gaudy jewelled pin, and a corresponding scarlet patch of lacy cloth that I took to be a handkerchief protruding from his breast pocket, added splashes of colour to the otherwise austere black and white of his formal attire. A breath of fresh air somehow seemed to fill the somewhat tobacco-laden atmosphere of our room.

"Sit down," said Holmes, waving him to an empty chair. "Pray indulge your habit of taking snuff if you wish. I will content myself with my pipe, with your permission. I trust your night in the Bow-street cells was not too uncomfortable ? "

I noticed the tell-tale smudges on the sleeve which told of our visitor's habits in the matter of tobacco, but I was at a loss as to how Holmes had arrived at the second conclusion. So, apparently, was our visitor.

"Mr. Holmes," he exclaimed in a heavy German accent. "I had heard of you as a magician, but how do you know of where I spent last night ? Why, I have not even told you my name ! I regret, by the way, not having being able to present you with my card upon my arrival here."

"My dear Professor Schinkenbein, I would be ignorant indeed if I did not recognise one of the great composers of the age. And as to your whereabouts, they are, I fear, a matter of public record," picking up the newspaper, and displaying the relevant article to the astonished musician.

The professor put his head in his hands. "My contract," he wailed. "Now the management of Covent Garden will never ask me to conduct there again. My career in this country is ruined. Maybe in every country in Europe. And all because of that damnable Persano." His voice rose to a shriek. "I should have never challenged him ! I should have shot him down on the spot like the dog he is ! " His voice cracked, and I had actually begun to fear for his sanity as he continued to rave in this manner. Indeed, I had risen from my seat, prepared to restrain him, should it become necessary to do so, when Holmes spoke.

"And with what reputation would you have emerged from such an affair ? " Holmes' quiet words acted like a glass of water thrown over the seemingly near-hysterical German, who suddenly ceased his ranting.

"You are quite correct, Mr. Holmes," he admitted, in a perfectly calm voice. "Of course it would be to no-one's advantage had I acted in such a fashion."

"Nonetheless," replied my friend, "though you acknowledge the truth of what I have just said to you, you still yearn for revenge, do you not ? " The German nodded. "And you are wondering if I will be the one to administer the revenge on your behalf ? " The musician once again gave his silent assent to Holmes' proposition. "My dear Professor, I have to tell you that, much as I may sympathise with you, and much as I may find myself in agreement with your position, it is neither my pleasure nor my place to go about the streets of London doling out summary punishment on behalf of my clients. Your work, Professor, when you stand on the concert platform in front of an orchestra, is carried out in here." Holmes tapped his head. "And so is mine. I am, as Watson here will tell you, not a man of action, but of thoughts." (Again I smiled inwardly, given the nature of our previous discussion.) "Should you wish me to solve a mystery for you, or should you ever do me the honour of inviting my violin and myself to take our place under your baton, I would be delighted to serve you in those regards, but I am not willing to put right your petty jealousies regarding matters which are, after all, a matter of artistic interpretation."

The musician flushed. "Mr. Holmes, I fear I have made a mistake in coming here. I had not expected to find the great detective so averse to a little practical matter."

"I fear I, too, was mistaken," replied Holmes, coolly. "When you came through the door, I was anticipating with pleasure the start of a friendship with a civilised man of culture. I regret that I, too, appear to have misjudged my acquaintance."

The professor flushed an even deeper red, and the veins on his forehead stood out as he rose to his feet. "Sir," he proclaimed in ringing tones. "I demand that you give me satisfaction."

Holmes' reply was a lazy laugh. "Professor, consider your reputation and your contract with Covent Garden," he sneered. "If you are worried that one challenge to a duel could have an adverse effect on your reputation, just consider what two such challenges in as many days would do."

"Pah ! " replied the other. "Upon reflection, I withdraw my challenge and wish both you gentlemen a very good day." So saying, he replaced his hat, and marched out of the door, closing it behind him with a definite bang.

"There ! That will hardly endear him to Mrs. Hudson," chuckled Holmes. "He did little to endear himself to me, I must confess. Why is it that men of such genius – and I freely admit that the man has the best grasp of any composer now living regarding the development of the theme of an aria – are such children when it comes to other matters ? "

"What was his true motive in visiting, do you think ? "

"Ah, so you remarked that, too ? 'Pon my word, Watson, you are coming on admirably." Such words from Holmes were not an everyday occurrence, and I felt myself well praised. "Your thoughts first, then ? "

"It is obvious that he is no physical coward. I noticed the scars of the German school of fencing which they practise at their universities, known as *Mensur*. I have witnessed such duels, and no man who is a coward would take part. I would therefore see no reason for his requesting you to take his place in this affair on that account, at the least."

"Good, Watson, good," he replied, rubbing his hands

together. " So far, we are in complete agreement."

" But beyond that, I fear I am puzzled," I confessed.

" Yes ? " replied Holmes. " So was I, I admit, until I noticed the direction of his gaze while he was venting his spleen towards the unfortunate critic."

" I failed to notice that. I was more concerned with his words and the state of his mental equilibrium."

" As he intended you to be," commented Holmes. " He was scanning my shelves, and his eyes came to rest on the portion of my bookcase that deals with the effects of poisons. No doubt you observed his spectacles ? "

" Gold-rimmed pince-nez," I confirmed.

" Indeed they are. But maybe you failed to remark the thickness of the lenses ? With such glasses, it would be easy for him to read the spines of the volumes on the shelf. Schinkenbein needs such in his work to observe the minute subtle details on the stage of the operas he conducts from the orchestra pit. I would venture to suggest that they are especially designed in some way to magnify his vision. Not only that, but Professor Schinkenbein's memory is renowned throughout Europe. He never conducts with a score, but keeps the whole of the opera, the notes and the libretto, in his head. It would be a trivial matter for him to commit to memory the titles and authors of the books there."

" To what end ? "

" Can you not guess ? The professor, as we have both observed, is no stranger to the art of the duello. He feels himself insulted by the unfortunate Persano's criticism, or maybe for some other reason as yet unknown to us, and requires satisfaction in the manner to which he is most accustomed. However, he has come to a country where such practices are frowned upon, and he finds himself in a position of public notoriety as a result of his impulses. I do not believe that this will result in the withdrawal of his contract with Covent Garden – indeed, I venture to predict that there will be no seats available for the next few weeks at least, as the public will want to view this fire-eating maestro with their own eyes. However, he still seeks his revenge, and, having heard of my reputation as possessing some small knowledge of the methods by which criminals achieve their ends, he decides that he will take advantage of my reputed expertise, without, as he fondly imagines, my being aware of his doing so."

"You mean that the critic Persano is now in danger of being poisoned by Professor Schinkenbein ? "

"I mean that Professor Schinkenbein currently believes that he will poison Persano. Whether he will actually attempt the deed or not is a matter for conjecture. In the event that he does so, I would venture to suggest that the attempt will fail. You will remember the Twickenham case last year, where the husband somehow failed to administer what was to have been a fatal dose of strychnine to his wife, missed his mark, and accordingly disposed of the neighbours' cat ? Poison is not the almighty tool that mere dabblers in crime believe it to be."

"But the professor is a man of learning and intelligence," I objected. "Surely it is unlikely that he would fall into the same error as the late Mr. Mallinson, whose wits, you must admit, were not of the sharpest ? "

"That is true," admitted Holmes. "All the same, I do not consider Persano to be in immediate danger from the quarter of the Professor."

"Why," I asked, as the thought occurred to me, "is Professor Schinkenbein currently at liberty, since he was taken into custody last night ? And do you believe that Persano is also now released from the cells ? "

"An excellent question, Watson." He scribbled a few lines on a piece of paper, and rang the bell for Mrs. Hudson. "Take this to the post-office, if you would be so kind, Mrs. Hudson. It should be sent reply-paid. There, that should give us our answer," he said, as the door closed behind our worthy landlady. "That is a telegram to Gregson at the Yard. Even if he is not in charge of the case, he owes me enough favours from the past to assist me."

The answer was received within the half-hour. "It would appear," said Holmes, reading the telegram that Mrs. Hudson presented to him, "that charges against both parties have been dropped. Both claim that words were spoken in the heat of the moment, and the influence of the grape was not absent."

"That hardly corresponds with what we saw just now, or indeed with what you observed," I remarked.

"You are correct there. I begin to fear a little more for Persano's safety. But there is nothing to be done at present about this matter. Indeed, I confess that it seems we are building this particular house upon sand, and there is little of import that we can do at this time."

T was some two weeks after the conversation described above that we received a visit from an unexpected source. The artistic director of Covent Garden Opera House, Mr. Daniel Tomlinson, sent a message to Holmes requesting him to visit him at his offices.

"You are going?" I asked Holmes, who appeared to be deep in the throes of some chemical experiment when the note was brought to him.

"Indeed we are going together," he replied. "This analysis is making damnably slow progress." He seized a glass beaker from the table that served as his laboratory bench, and tossed the contents into the fire, which leaped up with a brilliant green flame. "Copper," he observed sourly. "That much I knew before I started. Come, Watson. Bring your medical kit with you. If your Army revolver is to hand, you may also wish to equip yourself with that. I have a premonition that both of these may be of some use to us." I had no idea of his reasoning, but gripping my doctor's bag, in which a loaded revolver now lay incongruously beside a stethoscope, I followed Holmes into a hansom cab.

"Mr. Holmes, I am sorry to ask you here at considerable inconvenience, rather than meeting you at your own premises," apologised Mr. Tomlinson. "There are, to be frank, few times when I can be spared from my post here that are congenial to those of more conventional working hours." He was a tall slender man, whose thin ginger hair receded from a high forehead.

"I understand perfectly," smiled Holmes. "My own habits are not of the most regular, but I appreciate your consideration."

"To come to the point quickly," went on Tomlinson, "we are without a conductor for this evening's performance of the opera *Cosimo de Medici*."

"By Professor Paul Schinkenbein, who is also acting as the conductor ? " asked Holmes.

The other bowed slightly. "Indeed so. And it is Professor Schinkenbein who is missing at this moment."

"Surely the performance does not start for another two hours at least ? " I objected. "Could he not have been delayed, and he will appear in good time to direct the orchestra ? "

"Ordinarily, that would be the case," replied Tomlinson. "However, the Herr Professor, if I may term him so, is usually punctual to a Teutonic fault." There was a faint air of mockery in his tones, which vanished as he continued. "However, today he was due to be present here two hours ago. He had expressed his dissatisfaction to Signora Cantallevi, the soprano, regarding the phrasing of some of her solo arias, and he had arranged to work with her on these."

"He has forgotten his appointment ? " I suggested. "Or else he has simply overslept ? "

"I am afraid, Doctor, that we are ahead of you there. We

have already sent round to the hotel where he is lodging. Not only is he not at the hotel, but it would seem that he never appeared there following last night's performance. The porters do not recall seeing him enter the establishment, and when the maid went to his room this morning, it appeared that the bed had not been slept in."

"The name of the hotel ? " asked Holmes, and made a note of the reply on his shirt-cuff. His eyes glittered as he leaned forward. "Who was the last person to see him here in the theatre, do you know ? "

"That would be myself. I am not responsible for what we term the 'front of house' business – that is, the ticket receipts and so on – so when the stage has been cleared and the scene set for the next night's performance, I make a check of the green rooms and ensure that all the artistes are ready to leave, lest they be accidentally locked in the theatre. I am then myself free to leave. After last night's performance, which, I may tell you in confidence was not of the highest standards, especially the second half, Professor Schinkenbein was the only occupant of the green rooms. I reminded him of the time, and he dressed himself in his coat and hat, and accompanied me to the stage door, where we parted company."

"What time was this ? "

"Sixteen minutes past eleven by the Professor's watch, which is, as you might expect from such a man, accurate to the minute. He remarked on the time as we closed the stage door."

"Did you notice where he went after that ? " asked Holmes.

"I cannot swear to it, but I seem to have a memory of his summoning a hansom and entering it." He closed his eyes in a seeming aid to concentration. "Yes, indeed, that is what he did."

"He summoned a cab ? " enquired Holmes. "Would it not be more usual for him to make arrangements for a cab to be waiting for him ? "

Tomlinson frowned. " As you say, that was usually the case."

" Was he usually the last to leave ? " asked Holmes.

" By no means. Indeed, it was one of our little jokes among the staff here that it would be impossible for him to take an encore, as he would be in the cab driving home as the applause died away."

" So last night was exceptional ? Did he offer any explanation as to the change ? "

" None. I assumed, I suppose, that he had been working on today's proposed rehearsal with Signora Cantallevi."

" When did he and she agree on the arrangements for this rehearsal ? "

The other chuckled. " Mr. Holmes, I can assure you that 'agree' is hardly the term I would choose to apply to this matter. It was during last night's interval that the Professor stormed into Signora Cantallevi's dressing room and roared at her that she was murdering his music."

" He told you this ? "

" Not at all. Everyone backstage could hear his words. And I must confess, Mr. Holmes, that we theatre folk are somewhat fond of gossip. Everyone was listening intently to what was being said. Not that we could avoid hearing," he added hastily, " as neither the Professor nor the Signora is among the most discreet and unobtrusive of conversationalists."

" I think I understand the situation," said Holmes, with his characteristic half-smile. " So there would be no difficulty in confirming this ? "

" None whatsoever."

" The lady is of Italian extraction, I take it ? "

" As it happens, that is not the case," replied Tomlinson. " She assumed the stage name of Cantallevi some years ago, along with the Italian designation of Signora. She originally hails from South America—Uruguay or Argentina, if

I remember correctly. Her true name that appears on the contracts is Maria Muñoz."

"And where is the Signora now ? "

"In her dressing room. She is, if I am any judge at all of her character, extremely angry at being kept waiting. Patience, as well as tact, does not count among her virtues."

"Maybe it would be best if we were to visit the Professor's room first ? " suggested Holmes.

"If you wish. I had rather hoped, though, that you would be able to find the Professor himself."

"It is a capital mistake to theorise without data, as I have remarked to Watson on past occasions. At present, I lack sufficient data, and I wish to acquire such data as may be obtained from a study of the Professor's room. Following that, I may be in a position to help find the man himself."

Somewhat chastened, Tomlinson led the way through a maze of corridors lined with stage properties of all kinds, until we came to a door on which a neatly written card announced that the room was for the use of Herr Professor Paul Schinkenbein.

"Are these doors ever locked ? " asked Holmes, trying the door and pushing it open.

"Very occasionally," replied our host. "Maybe a singer has been given a valuable piece of jewellery from an admirer which she will be expected to wear when she meets the admirer after the performance... Sometimes the tenor or baritone will require, shall we say, a little privacy when visited by his admirers..." His voice tailed off, and he coughed. " I think, as a man of the world, you understand my meaning here ? "

"Of course," said Holmes. "I am aware of such matters in the world of the theatre. Did the Professor ever lock his door ? "

Tomlinson flushed. "Are you implying, sir..? "

"I merely enquired whether the Professor ever locked his door," replied Holmes, mildly.

" He commenced the habit some three or four weeks back. Before that, his door was always left unlocked. It was unlocked last night when I was making my final rounds."

"And on those occasions when his door was locked, Signora Cantallevi was not to be seen elsewhere in the theatre, I take it ? No, no, you need not answer that question, as your face has told me everything. Rest assured that you have said nothing to me that can be interpreted as being to the discredit of either party. Let us move on to another subject. When you met the Professor last night, did he tidy away any papers before you and he left the room ? "

" I have no recollection of his doing so."

" And yet you believed he was working on today's projected rehearsal ? "

" My belief only. He never said so outright."

Holmes stooped to the floor and retrieved a scrap of paper. He held it up for us to examine, but I could make little of it. It appeared to be a piece of ordinary brown paper, such as is used to wrap parcels. The letters " INA" were printed in white on the red corner of a postage stamp that adhered to one torn edge.

" Does the Professor smoke ? " asked Holmes. " I know for a fact that he is a snuff-taker."

" I have never observed him smoking."

" Strange, strange..." Holmes muttered to himself, looking at a line of at least twenty matchboxes on the dressing table. " Watson, what do you notice about these ? "

" They are all of different brands. I see no duplicates here."

" Nor I. Furthermore, all these are of subtly different sizes, if you will observe, arranged with German precision from left to right in order of their overall size."

" There is a gap there, towards the right," I remarked.

" Indeed," said Holmes. " I would wager that the Professor has that missing box in his possession at this very moment."

" Mr. Holmes," called the theatre manager. " Look here."
He pointed to the waste-paper basket, which was full of live
matches.

" At least twenty boxes' worth, I would say," remarked
Holmes. " When are these baskets emptied ? "

" Three times weekly. In fact," he pulled out his watch,
" probably within the next hour."

" Why on earth would someone go to this trouble to procure an empty matchbox of such precise dimensions ? " I
wondered aloud. Holmes said nothing in reply, but raised
his eyebrows.

" What other surprises has the Professor left for us ? " he
asked, rhetorically, casting about the room.

I noticed what appeared to be some cotton wool with the
matches, matted in places with a curious green material,
seemingly liquid that had dried, and I called Holmes' attention to it.

" Good, Watson, good. Would you have the goodness to
use the forceps from your medical bag to remove it, and
place it in this envelope ? Thank you. And I would advise
sterilising those forceps before they touch your next patient,
Doctor." I remembered the Professor's apparent interest in
poisons, and shuddered.

" Now," remarked Holmes, " for our prima donna. I
somehow doubt her current willingness to receive visitors."

We had reached the singer's door, and Tomlinson rapped
smartly on it.

" Enter," came the imperious command. The singer was
standing in the middle of the room. A beauty of the Latin
type, her dark eyes flashed angry fire at us as we entered.

Tomlinson introduced Holmes and myself to the singer,
who surveyed us with a critical eye. " You, I have heard
of," she addressed Holmes. " You are the man who finds
things, no ? I tell you, I do not want you to find the pig of
a Professor Schinkenbein. I do not care if I never see his
ugly face again. Whatever he was to me in the past, he is

nothing to me now. Nothing, I tell you, nothing ! "

Holmes started to reply, but was seized by a fit of coughing. "Excuse me," he apologised, as he retrieved a throat pastille from his pocket and unwrapped it, before putting it into his mouth. He indicated the wrapping that he still held in his hand, and the soprano waved a languid arm in the direction of the waste-paper basket in the corner. Holmes walked over and deposited the paper there before returning to the centre of the room. Unseen by any except me, he palmed a few scraps of paper from the basket and placed them unobtrusively in his pocket.

"I fear, Signora," Holmes addressed the diva with grave courtesy, "that we have disturbed you unnecessarily. My apologies." He sketched a bow, and backed out of the room.

"I was under the impression that you wished to talk with her," said Tomlinson.

"I have seen and heard all I needed," replied Holmes. "And besides," shrugging, "she does not seem in the mood for conversation. Come, Watson, I believe we have learned all we can here for the present."

THINK we now have the threads, Watson," Holmes remarked to me as we sat in the cab transporting us to the hotel where Professor Schinkenbein had been lodging. "I begin to believe that we are now on the trail of a case that may prove to be of more than average interest in the details, however mundane the basic facts."

"I confess that I am still in the dark," I replied. "I have, however, drawn my own conclusions regarding the relations between the Professor and Signora Cantallevi. I find it hard to believe, though, that a man of such gifts as the Professor could behave in such an immoral fashion."

Holmes turned to me with a half-smile on his lips. "Watson, you are the very rock of British respectability itself, but you must learn to make allowances for the artistic temperament. Geniuses such as Schinkenbein are not bound by the mundane trappings of everyday folk. In any event, I had established that there was a lady in the case two weeks ago."

"But that was before we were even aware there was any case to be examined," I objected. "And how could you possibly know such a thing ? "

For answer, Holmes merely gave me an enigmatic smile.

"What was the paper you retrieved from the Signora's dressing room ? " I asked him.

"Ah, you noticed my little sleight of hand, did you ? " he replied. "See for yourself."

The papers consisted of several scraps of a photograph, which had been ripped to shreds. Two of the fragments bore traces of handwriting, which might well have been an autograph.

"My money, were I a betting man, Watson, would be on this having been a photograph of Professor Schinkenbein," he remarked as the cab drew up at the hotel.

"Would it be possible for me to examine the rooms in which Professor Schinkenbein has been staying ? " enquired Holmes of the hotel's manager, who had received us in his office.

"In the usual run of things, I would be compelled to refuse such a request," replied the other. "Since you have done us so many good turns in the past and saved the good name of the hotel from scandal, I cannot refuse you this, Mr. Holmes."

"I am confident that no breath of scandal can attach itself to the hotel in this case," Holmes assured him. "I merely need to ascertain a few facts. Have the rooms been cleaned since the Professor last entered them ? "

"Almost certainly."

Holmes' face clouded. "No matter," he replied. "Would you have the goodness to have me shown up there ? "

The manager pressed a bell, and one of the porters led us up the stairs to the missing Professor's apartments.

"Ha ! " exclaimed Holmes. "I fear that the hotel staff have been too busy for us to discover anything of value." He peered about the bed-room, lifting the bed-cover and looking under the bed. "Ha ! What is this ? " He reached under the bed, and withdrew a small scrap of brown paper.

"The same kind of paper that we found in his room in Covent Garden ? " I asked.

"I believe so," replied Holmes, withdrawing it from his pocket and laying it side by side with the scrap he had just discovered. "Yes, they match perfectly. And what's this ? " pointing to a few handwritten letters.

I read, neatly printed in black ink, what appeared to be the ends of a few lines of address:

> "*...uñoz*
> *...illa de Correro 419*
> *...ro Central*
> *...s Aires*
> *...ENTINA*"

"Clear enough, wouldn't you say, Watson ? "

I thought for a moment. "He received a package from Argentina ? "

"Of course, Watson. And Signora Cantallevi's true name ? "

"Muñoz, of course," I recalled.

"My Spanish is a little less than fluent, but it would seem to me, Watson, that what we have in front of us here is the fragment of the return address written on a package sent to the Professor by a relative of the singer. I would venture to suggest that the second line originally read 'Casilla de Correro 419', the Spanish for *poste restante*, at the central post office, 'Correro', in Buenos Aires. Add this to the fragment of Argentinian stamp that adhered to this scrap of paper that we found in the dressing room, and I think there can be no doubt."

"But what could the Professor possibly want with a package from Argentina ? What could it possibly contain ? "

"Something that would fit inside a certain matchbox," replied Holmes enigmatically. "And I begin to fear the worst."

"I hardly know what you mean by this," I shuddered.

"I hardly know myself," confessed Holmes, "but I fear we are on the trail of some devilment."

Holmes continued to search the bed-room and sitting-room in his typical fashion that appeared almost absent-minded, but in truth missed nothing. At length he turned to me and sighed. "Nothing more. The housekeepers at this hotel carry out their appointed tasks too well," he complained. "Believe me, half the unsolved crimes of London would remain unsolved no longer, if the housekeepers of this world were not so desirous of removing every alien object, and scrubbing and polishing every surface in sight."

We went downstairs and re-entered the manager's office.

"May I talk to the staff who deal with your guests' post ? "

"Of course," replied the manager. "I trust that your inspection of the room was fruitful ? "

"Indeed it was," Holmes assented, "though I suppose that I must compliment you on the efficiency of your staff, who make the work of a detective such as myself more difficult than it need be."

The elderly porter responsible for sorting and delivering the hotel guests' post entered the office.

"Simpson, you have my full permission to answer any questions these gentlemen may see fit to put to you," the manager told him.

"Thank you," said Holmes. "Now, Simpson, my questions are concerned only with those items addressed to Professor Schinkenbein. Did you receive any special instructions from the Professor regarding these ? "

"Why yes, sir, I did. I have never heard of anything like it from any of our other guests, but the Professor told me that if there was to be any letters or packages addressed to him from South America—Argentina, or those parts—I was not to deliver them to his room, but to forward them to another address."

Holmes sat forward in his chair. "Is that address in London ? " he asked.

"Yes, sir, that it is. I have it written down here, sir, in this book of mine," he explained, drawing a tattered notebook from an inside pocket of his uniform.

"Aha ! " exclaimed Holmes, examining the relevant page. "You and I, Watson, must lose no time in visiting number 23, Brixham Gardens."

 RIXHAM Gardens turned out to be a dreary row of red-brick houses in North Hampstead, bounded at the back by the railway, with the small park that gave the street its name at one end of the street.

"I wonder why he chose this area as his little hideaway," Holmes wondered aloud.

"Perhaps it is near to Miss Muñoz' dwelling ? " I suggested.

Holmes clapped his hands together. "There are occasions, Watson, when you positively sparkle. I am sure you have hit on something very close to the truth."

We paid off the cab, and rang the bell of number 23. There was no answer, but we could hear some sort of laughter from within.

"There is someone at home," I remarked, "but they seem unwilling to answer the door."

"Or else they are unable to do so," replied Holmes, enigmatically.

"Let us break down the door and enter, if you fear foul

play."

"You underestimate my skills as a housebreaker," Holmes reproached me. So saying, he went to the side of the house, leaving me standing guard outside the front door. I had just raised my hand to ring the bell once more, when the door opened, and Holmes let me into the hall. His face was grave.

"I fear the worst," he said to me in a low tone. The laughter we had heard earlier came from upstairs, and now we could hear it more clearly, sounded disjointed and, if such a word can be used of laughter, irrational.

"Your revolver, Watson," Holmes advised me, as we mounted the stairs. I withdrew it from its unaccustomed resting-place in my medical bag, and gripped it tightly in my right hand.

"Here, I think," whispered Holmes in a low voice, pausing outside a closed door. "On my word, Watson. One... two..."

On "three" he wrenched open the door and flung it wide.

Never in my life have I beheld such a sight. The room was bare of all furniture, save a deal table and two chairs. In one chair sat the body of Professor Schinkenbein, naked from the waist upward, with a hideous rictal sneer on his face. His garments were strewn around the floor. A mere glance was sufficient to tell me that life had fled the body some time before.

"The poor devil," whispered Holmes. "The poor devil," he repeated softly.

Our gaze was torn from the hideous sight of the deceased composer by the other man in the room, whom I recognised as Isadora Persano, the journalist, and erstwhile challenger of the Professor. He was seated at the other chair facing the Professor, and he stared at us, wide-eyed.

"No more, no more, you shut the door, and then no more," he remarked to me, in a conversational tone. "You mount the grade, without my aid, though you're afraid, and won't be stayed."

"What the deuce do you mean by that ? " I asked him. Holmes laid a hand on my sleeve.

"I fear the poor fellow's wits have deserted him," Holmes said.

As if to confirm this, Persano burst into song. "And the little pigs sing, ring-a-ding, ring-a-ding," he carolled gaily to us as we approached him.

"No ! As you value your sanity ! " Holmes spoke to me in a hoarse urgent whisper, as I reached out my hand to the half-open matchbox that stood on the table in front of the unfortunate lunatic. "Look from a safe distance, if you must, but do not touch."

I peered at the opening, and the hideous pink fleshy head of some vile worm-like creature emerged. Some kind of green liquid drooled from what I took to be its jaws.

"What is it, Holmes ? " I gasped.

"I know not, and I care not," he replied. If I have ever seen Sherlock Holmes afraid, it was on that occasion. The blood had drained from his face, and his jaw was set. He masked his face with a handkerchief so that only his eyes were visible, and drew on his gloves. "Have the kindness, Doctor, to pass me your longest pair of forceps, and if you have such a thing as a specimen jar for the collection of bodily fluids, I would welcome the loan of that as well."

I passed him the required utensils, and he deftly captured the creature, removing it from the box, and transferred it to the jar. It feebly spat the green fluid in his general direction, but seemed to lack the strength to reach him with its vile spittle.

"I am relieved to see that it lacks an infinite supply of this hellish fluid," remarked Holmes, screwing on the lid of the jar with his gloved hands. The worm writhed inside the jar, still spitting feebly. Now we could see it, it appeared to be about four inches long, as thick as a child's finger, and as pink. The face, if it may be so described, appeared grotesque and almost evil in its aspect.

"And now, if you have morphia or some other such drug in that bag of yours, I would advise that you administer it to this poor fellow here," said Holmes, "while I summon the police and the lunatic asylum."

  HAD my suspicions," remarked Holmes, when I discussed the case with him later, "almost from the start. It was when we visited Covent Garden and discovered the Professor's attachment to Miss Muñoz that my vague fears became more concrete. Of course, I knew that the fair sex was involved from the beginning when Schinkenbein first visited us."

"How did you know there was a lady in the case ? " I asked Holmes.

"Elementary. I observed a strong odour of feminine perfume when he entered the room. It was not the kind of scent that I could imagine being used by any man, no matter how artistic his temperament. It was obvious that he had been in recent close, if not actually intimate, contact with a young lady of looser morality than the kind of which you would approve, Watson," he wagged a finger at me, "in the past twenty-four hours."

"I bow to your superior reasoning here," I replied.

"Surely you also observed the oddities in his attire when he visited our rooms ? " Holmes asked me.

"I remember the cravat, the topaz scarf-pin and the scarlet lace handkerchief," I replied.

Holmes laughed out loud. "That, my dear Watson, was no handkerchief. Had you examined it more closely, you would have identified it as a lady's garter."

I confess I blushed. "What sort of blackguard would parade himself in society with such an intimate item so prominently visible ? I suppose we can take it for granted that this was not a sentimental memento of the Professor's wife ? "

" According to my sources, his wife – or should we say his widow – is a somewhat elderly German *Hausfrau*, currently residing at the family home in Berlin, and is hardly the type of lady to wear such garments. No, I am sure that the open display of such an object was intended as some sort of trophy signifying his conquest of the lady in question, of whose identity we are already in no doubt."

" The utter cad ! " I exclaimed. " The world is well rid of him."

" From the viewpoint of today's morality, you may well be correct there," Holmes admitted. " But he is a sad loss to the world of opera."

Once again, I found myself in silent disagreement with my friend's eccentricity in the matter of morals.

" I can guess a little," I replied. " Persano and Muñoz arrived together in this country from Argentina as lovers."

" That much I have ascertained from other quarters," he affirmed.

" And she subsequently transferred her affections to Professor Schinkenbein. This aroused the ire of the slighted Persano, who took his revenge in the form of his criticism of Schinkenbein's music."

" Excellent, Watson. Your intuition and judgement when it comes to affairs of the heart are truly admirable." I flushed a little. " However, when it comes to the truly rational aspects of these matters..." He shook his head sadly.

I continued, a little abashed. " I would suggest that the supposed subject of the public quarrel in the restaurant was a pretext for a challenge over Miss Muñoz."

" Something along those lines, I agree. Certainly, all was not as appeared at first sight in that incident, I am sure."

" After that, I am unsure of the course of events."

" I am reasonably certain that the original intention of fighting a duel was a serious one on both sides," said

Holmes. "Both had something of a reputation in their own countries as duellists, and neither was lacking in physical courage. Their arrest and subsequent detention must have brought home to them that such a course of action was not practicable in this country."

"And at this point, we had our visit from the Professor ? "

"Indeed. He was probably examining my shelves for methods of poisoning with serious intent, but I feel he may have been laying his murderous plans even before that time. The package containing the worm was dispatched from Argentina by Miss Muñoz' relation – a brother, maybe, but it is unimportant – before the incident of the threatened duel. I am guessing that her former paramour was continuing to importune Miss Muñoz against her wishes, and she, too, wished to see his demise. It would be easy for her to acquire some sort of exotic means of death from her own country that would baffle our English authorities."

"And the worm ? What of that ? "

"The Natural History Museum in South Kensington has been unable to identify it. The green spittle has been analysed, and is confirmed as containing a powerful alkaloid with varying effects on its subjects when absorbed through the skin. For some it causes failure of the respiratory system, but others seem relatively unaffected in that regard. However, it in every case it appears to exercise a powerful effect on that part of the circulatory system that leads to the brain, leading to a loss of mental faculties, as we saw in the case of poor Persano, and most probably the Professor as well before his death."

"I can vaguely understand the reasons why Schinkenbein would want to encompass the death of Persano, given the goads that resulted from the criticism of his work. But how did he meet his own end ? "

"I would have thought you could have deduced that yourself, Watson. When Schinkenbein ventured to criticise the phrasing of the diva's arias, all passion fled. You saw her reaction to his name for yourself, and you also handled the fragments of his inscribed photograph which she had ripped to shreds in her fury."

" And the rejected lover decided to take his own life ? "

" I believe so. We have been fortunate that the authorities have been willing to accept a verdict of accidental death, and his widow will suffer no loss of reputation. My belief is that he first goaded the worm into releasing its foul liquid on himself, and in his last moments of sanity, passed the matchbox to Persano."

" The matchbox still puzzles me, I confess. Why was that matchbox missing from the line, and why were all the other matchboxes in his room in the first instance ? "

Holmes smiled. " I do not know, and I can only make a guess here. The original intention was to present Persano with a matchbox containing the worm, exchanging it for the box of matches which Persano carried with him to light his cigars. The problem with this plan was that the match-box had to be of the same brand as Persano's customary matches."

" So that was the meaning of the collection of matchboxes that we discovered ? " I asked.

" Precisely. My surmise here is that Miss Muñoz was un-able to recollect Persano's habits precisely, and the differ-ent types of match were purchased by Schinkenbein as an aide-memoire. The fact that they were arranged in order of size is a tribute to Schinkenbein's Teutonic sense of neat-ness and precision, rather than on account of any practical reason. Hence my amusement at the time when you men-tioned the size of the matchbox."

" You had obtained the solution at that stage ? "

" I was close to a solution, but lacked the closing evi-dence. What we subsequently learned at the hotel filled the gaps in my knowledge."

" It sounds plausible, at the very least," I replied.

" I think it is more than plausible; it is probable," he

replied. "I have no wish to rake up more scandal by asking questions of Miss Muñoz, and it fits the facts as we know them."

"A sad affair," I remarked.

"Indeed. I must admit, looking on this business, that there may be something to be said for your conventional ideas of morality, Watson, if disregard of the same can bring about such consequences. On the other hand," he added, turning to his violin, "our lives would be less interesting if everyone shared your beliefs."

So saying, he started to saw away at his fiddle in a tune I recognized as one of the arias from the late Professor Paul Schinkenbein's *Cosimo de Medici*.

The Case of the

Cormorant

"We stood together in silence, gazing across the bay to St. Mawes and St. Anthony Head, with its famous white-painted lighthouse at the foot." (page 66)

EDITOR'S NOTE

In The Veiled Lodger, *Dr. Watson states:*

"*I deprecate, however, in the strongest way the attempts which have been made lately to get at and to destroy these papers. The source of these outrages is known, and if they are repeated I have Mr. Holmes' authority for saying that the whole story concerning the politician, the lighthouse, and the trained cormorant will be given to the public. There is at least one reader who will understand.*"

This cryptic utterance has baffled students of Holmes' history and cases for many years. The story alluded to was, for a long time, considered to be unwritten, existing only in the memory of Holmes (and possibly Watson), and the facts held in reserve against the possibility of an attack on Watson's records as described above.

It was with great pleasure, therefore, that the following account was discovered in the deed box which had once been the property of John Watson, MD. The MS had been carefully placed in not just one, but three stout manila envelopes, each sealed with the impression of two signet rings, one of which bore the initials "SH" and the other a simple "W". The outermost bore the words, "The Case of the Cormorant", and this is the title by which I now make this available to the world.

Y friend Sherlock Holmes had been suffering from a surfeit of cases which admitted of no easy solution, and which had at the last caused a seeming debilitation of even his apparently indestructible faculties. As his friend and his medical adviser, I persuaded him that a temporary retreat from the metropolis was in the best interests of his health and he assented with an alacrity which somewhat surprised me.

My suggestions that we spend a week enjoying the pleasures of the Normandy coast at Deauville or some similar watering place did not meet with his approval, however, and he proposed as an alternative that we travel to the westernmost county of our principal island—Cornwall. I was happy to fall in with this idea, and welcomed the prospect of bracing walks along the rugged coastline of that most entrancing, and in many ways one of the most mysterious, of counties.

Accordingly, we reserved rooms, assembled our garments and other accoutrements necessary for a stay in the countryside, and travelled on the express train from Paddington Station to Falmouth. Upon arrival, we enquired as to the whereabouts of the lodgings where we had secured accommodation, and on finding that they were close by, Holmes proposed stretching our legs after the train journey by walking to our destination, and sending our luggage on by trap. The plan seemed to me to be a good one, and we strolled through the streets of the charming old town, taking in the quaintnesses and sights as we did so. By the time we had reached the home of our landlady, Mrs. Buncombe, I for one felt no pangs of regret at the decision to remain in our native land rather than making a journey to foreign parts.

Holmes seemed indifferent to the natural beauties of the surrounding countryside, as he did to the man-made interests of the place, but contented himself with an examination of the plants and vegetation growing along the hedgerows, occasionally referring to a small handbook on such matters that he carried in his pocket.

After our welcome by Mrs. Buncombe, we found ourselves seated in her guest drawing room, where on a polished table before us stood a tea-tray, brought in to us by our smiling landlady. On this in turn stood a steaming teapot, and scones served with the finest Cornish cream and jam which had its origins, so Mrs. Buncombe had assured us, in the wild strawberries growing in the area, Holmes stretched his legs to their fullest extent, and sighed with what appeared to be genuine pleasure.

"I foresee an interesting week here, Watson," he remarked to me.

"By 'interesting', I take it you mean 'relaxing', do you not ? I am delighted to see you taking an interest in some of the glories of nature, rather than the sins of your fellow man, but I feel you should at some time in the coming days lift your eyes somewhat in order to appreciate the beauties of the whole landscape, rather than the individual plants that compose it."

"By no means do I intend to allow myself to become sunk in idleness, Watson, but I will, even so, attempt to avail myself of the opportunities for mental refreshment to which you allude. However, at this juncture, the matter of physical refreshment would appear to be of more importance." So saying, he proffered the plate of scones to me, taking two of them for himself and placing them on his plate. I feared for my friend's continuing health if he continued to refuse to allow himself to unwind, if the process of prolonged mental relaxation may so be described, but determined to hold my peace for the nonce.

 WAS awakened early the next morning by the sound of gunfire from outside the window of the room I was sharing with Holmes. I turned to alert Holmes of the fact, but the other bed was unoccupied. Glancing at my watch and noting the time, as my association with Holmes had trained me to do as a matter of course, I hurriedly pulled on some clothes and made my way downstairs, where I let myself out through the back door of the house, which was unlocked.

On arrival at the small orchard at the rear of the house, I encountered Sherlock Holmes, calmly reloading his revolver with fresh ammunition. A row of bottles which had once contained beer stood on a sawhorse some ten yards away, with the necks of the leftmost six bottles shattered.

" Holmes ! " I expostulated. " This is intolerable ! Revolver practice at the hour of half past five in the morning is not only eccentric in the extreme, but positively inconsiderate of others. I would experience no surprise if Mrs. Buncombe, who is, I would remind you, an elderly widow living alone except for any lodgers, decided to throw us out of the house forthwith and invited us to make our way back to London."

Holmes regarded me, a faint smile on his lips. " Watson, you serve as my guide and conscience in these matters. I do confess that the further implications of this little exercise of mine had slipped my mind. I awoke to the unaccustomed sound of birdsong, and a likewise unfamiliar vista of green leaves, and decided to avail myself of the solitude afforded by the early hour. On encountering these bottles, it occurred to me that this would be a suitable occasion to renew my skills with the revolver. I seem to remember your expressing displeasure at my doing so in our rooms at Baker-street at one time."

" Quite so, Holmes. There is a time and a place for such an exercise, and half-past five in the morning is no time, and the interior of our rooms in London is no place." I spoke with some heat.

" Tush, Watson. I fear you are quite vexed."

" I am indeed. I would suggest that you apologize to Mrs. Buncombe at the earliest possible opportunity, and that you and I work together now to remove and dispose of any broken glass, which will undoubtedly pose a danger to any passers-by."

"Very good. As you say." Holmes pocketed his revolver, after, I was happy to note, first removing the cartridges from the cylinder. "I will indeed extend my apologies to our worthy landlady at the first possible opportunity, and we will dispose of the *débris* that I have created. Ah—"

Mrs. Buncombe had appeared in the back doorway of the house, and was staring at us across the orchard. Holmes and I walked to meet her. I was pleased to see Holmes' stride appear a little less confident than usual, and I had hopes that my words might have had some lasting effect on him.

As we approached Mrs. Buncombe, Holmes, who had opened his mouth to speak, was forestalled by the good lady herself.

"Did either of you two gentlemen happen to hear that Jim Pollard shooting at them crows ? " she enquired of us. "He ought to be stopped from doing such a thing of an early morning. It's not a fit practice for Christian folk to be out killing the Lord's creatures at that hour. Deaf as I may be, the sound of that dratted gun, if you'll forgive the word, woke me up out of my bed."

Holmes and I exchanged glances. Holmes, I could guess from my past experience of his moods, was struggling to contain his laughter, so I replied in his place.

"Indeed we did, Mrs. Buncombe, but we saw nothing." I spoke loudly and distinctly. As we had discovered the previous day, and as she had admitted to us herself, the good lady's hearing was not of the keenest. Holmes had turned away, seemingly seized with a violent fit of coughing.

"Well, I must thank you two gentlemen for taking the trouble to see what was going on. Since I am alone in the house as a rule, it is a comfort to me to know that you are here," she replied. "And since you are both up and doing, it seems to me that a cup of tea would be welcome."

"Thank you, Mrs. Buncombe," I replied. "You are quite correct in your surmise."

"Then I will just be running along and putting the kettle on. I will call you when your tea is ready, if you want to stay outside a little longer."

As she made her way to her domestic mysteries, I turned to Holmes. "We were lucky that time, Holmes," I said as sternly as I could manage. "We must give thanks to Jim Pollard, whoever he may be, for his unconscious intervention in our affairs."

"Indeed so," said Holmes. "Come, let us carry out your excellent suggestion of clearing away the remnants of my targets."

As we carefully collected the glass fragments and placed them in a wooden seed-tray, he remarked to me, "Do you remark anything strange about these bottles?"

"Not that I have noticed. I assume that you have done so?"

He nodded. "There are several noteworthy points. The first is that of their very existence. If you remember at last night's excellent dinner, Mrs. Buncombe, when she presented us with a bottle of claret as an accompaniment to the roast shoulder of lamb, remarked that she was Temperance, and that alcohol never passed her own lips, though she was not averse to her lodgers partaking of the same."

"True, but these bottles could be the leavings of the libations of previous lodgers?"

"A neat alliteration, Watson," he remarked. "Naturally that possibility had occurred to me. However, many of the bottles retain the familiar aroma of good English beer, which would seem to argue that they were emptied relatively recently. In addition, I think we have both observed that our Mrs. Buncombe is clean and tidy to a fault. If these bottles were the leavings of previous guests, I do not believe she would have left them behind that tool-shed yonder, and even had she done so, she would certainly have washed them clean before placing them there."

I considered this for a moment. "The solution is simple, Holmes," I replied. "These bottles are the result of her gardener, or some outside servant, refreshing himself in the intervals of his toil."

Holmes shook his head. "I fear you are mistaken. Though that thought also crossed my mind, it is not borne out by the bottles themselves. Observe that there are many different brews represented here. You must have remarked for yourself that when it comes to beer, the English workman is a creature of habit. Take from him his usual tipple, and he will be unhappy with any substitute, even if he cannot tell, blindfolded, the difference between the products of different breweries. In addition, the labels on these bottles indicate that their sources are from a wider geography than I would expect to be represented by the establishments of this town."

Holmes' observation appeared to be correct; on inspection, there hardly seemed to be two bottles the same, with some even having their origin in the neighbouring county of Devon. "Your conclusion, then ? "

"This garden is employed as a meeting-place by a number of individuals, who assemble here from a number of diverse locations, and spend some time here—at any rate, a length of time which allows them to enjoy a companionable drink together. Observe," he remarked, leading me down a slight slope away from the house towards a small cove. The orchard extended nearly to the shore, which consisted at this point of a sandy beach. "From here, we are invisible, except from the sea, and that from only the one angle. The trees on either side of this inlet prevent observation from elsewhere. And, confirming my surmise..." he stooped and picked up the end of a cigar from the ground. "I hardly think that this would be one of Mrs. Buncombe's leavings, nor yet one of her gardener's. This is the remains of a truly noble product of Havana – one which I would expect to be enjoyed only by one of the more well-to-do members of our society." He placed the remnant in one of the envelopes with which he was always provided. "And furthermore," he added, "the gentleman suffers from the defect of a missing right incisor. Such a person should be easy to identify in this rural spot. There cannot be many such here."

We were interrupted in our conversation by the sound of Mrs. Buncombe's voice coming from the house. "There is something that is not as it should be," said Holmes, as we turned and walked back towards the house with its promise of good cheer in the shape of a cup of tea. "I cannot for the moment ascertain its exact nature, but believe me, I sense its presence lurking."

Such dark thoughts were at odds with the blue skies and verdant landscape, edged by the sea, that surrounded us, and I determined to direct Holmes' thoughts to happier things as soon as possible.

ITH this object in mind, I persuaded Holmes to accompany me on a walk to the famous Pendennis Castle, originally built by our Bluff King Hal to protect the realm from invasion. The view from the headland on which the castle stands is truly magnificent, and we stood together in silence, gazing across the bay to St. Mawes and St. Anthony Head, with its famous white-painted lighthouse at the foot.

Holmes stood, seemingly drinking in the view by my side, but to someone who knew him as well as myself, it was clear that the beauty of his surroundings was far from being the principal object of his thoughts. This was confirmed with his next words to me.

"The lighthouse was visible from the point where we discovered the cigar end, was it not?" This was hardly a question requiring a reply, and I refrained from answering.

Holmes continued his musings. "And yet, if I am right, it would not be visible from the house, nor yet from any other place nearby, as the trees would block the view. We will have to return and investigate – later, Watson, later, not now," as I started to expostulate.

"What is the significance of this ? " I asked him. "Indeed, is it likely that there is any significance at all ? "

"I do not know," he replied. "I find it curious, that is all, that a diverse group of men should assemble from where the one spot where the lighthouse is easily seen, and which is in its turn almost invisible from other points."

"Smugglers ? " I suggested, my imagination having been fired by a history of these men which I had recently been reading.

"This is hardly a time when bales of French lace and the like would make it worthwhile running the gauntlet of Her Majesty's Excisemen," Holmes replied. "In any event, landing any such cargo, be it lace, spirits, or tobacco, would seem to demand that such goods be transported elsewhere. There are no roads leading to that place, and I saw no signs of any heavy loads being moved."

"Perhaps the smugglers arrive by boat and depart using the same method ? " I suggested.

"That strikes me as being quite possible," said Holmes. "If I recall the breweries of the beer originally contained in those bottles, each one of them is located in a coastal town, if not a port. So, Watson, we have a secretive band of men, beer-drinkers from different ports of the West Country, chiefly this county, arriving by boat, converging on one spot from which they can only be seen by that lighthouse over there, and presumably departing the way they have come. What does that say to you ? "

"I can only think of smuggling at present."

"I as well," he confessed. "But it does not ring true to me at all. Why would smugglers choose such a place, rather than meeting some distance from the shore and transferring the goods in mid-ocean, where the rule of the excisemen is less likely to be enforced ? Also, the boats used to transport the goods must be small—the water is shallow near that place, and a large boat would have difficulty in drawing near. It would hardly appear to be worth a smuggler's while to risk several years of imprisonment for a dinghy's worth of brandy."

" But if the cargo were something relatively small, but yet valuable ? " I ventured.

"Indeed, Watson ! Bravo ! I do believe that you may have something there," he congratulated me. " It is hard to think what such a commodity might be, though ? "

" Pearls ? " I hazarded, my thoughts still running along maritime lines.

Holmes shook his head. " I doubt that to be the case. Pearls are not commonly reckoned to be among the principal products of this county. Likewise, I doubt any kind of jewels, though they would likewise meet the criteria you established. My observations would seem to indicate that such meetings have taken place several times over the past few months, and it is impossible that there would be a steady supply of such articles to supply the number of carriers I deduce to have been present. I am at present unable to consider any alternative, though."

" Let us return for luncheon," I suggested. " Mrs. Buncombe gave us to understand that a grilled mackerel apiece would feature as the main dish, and it is a fish of which I am particularly fond."

FTER luncheon, which lived up to my expectations, I retired to our room. My early rising, which had been occasioned by Holmes' eccentric revolver practice, followed by the walk and the sea air, had left me a little sleepy, and I resolved to take what our Mediterranean cousins term a *siesta*, a practice which, incidentally, I had often followed in my service in India.

It was with a slight sense of relief that I removed my boots and laid myself on the bed. It seemed, though, that I had hardly closed my eyes when there was a loud knock at the door.

"Doctor Watson ! " came the voice of Mrs. Buncombe. "If you would be kind enough to help, sir ? "

I got up and opened the door.

"I wouldn't have disturbed you, sir, excepting that it was urgent, but it's young Harry Tregeare. He's come over all queer, and Doctor Pengelly is over at St. Mawes right now."

"Very good, Mrs. Buncombe. Please give me a few minutes to make myself ready and I will be with you." I laced up my boots and splashed cold water from the jug over my face. Happily I had thought to bring along my medical bag, which contained the usual apparatus appropriate to my calling.

"Where is the patient ? " I asked Mrs. Buncombe, who was waiting anxiously at the bottom of the stairs. Holmes was nowhere to be seen.

"He's at the 'Lion'," she told me. "In the public bar. But Jim Stott – he's the landlord there – says it's not the drink. He'd only just touched his beer – Harry Tregeare, that is – when he came over all strange."

She led me along the street to the public house, a quaint old-fashioned building. "The door's there," she pointed. "I'm not going in there. I took my oath I would never enter one of those places, and even for Harry Tregeare, I'm not going to break my word."

I lifted the latch of the barroom door and entered. There were perhaps a dozen customers in there, mostly fisherman from their appearance, and they were clustered around a wooden settle on which lay a young man.

"You are the doctor, then ? " asked a stout man wearing a white apron, presumably the landlord of the establishment.

"I am indeed. And this, I take it, is my patient ? " indicating the recumbent figure.

The others made space for me as I approached and started my examination of the young man, who appeared to be unconscious. "Do you have a cushion or something similar we can place under his head ? " I asked the landlord. "It is not merely for his comfort, but I have no wish for his respiratory faculties to be temporarily incapacitated." The use of such language, as I had hoped, seemed to inspire some respect among the onlookers, and a cushion was speedily produced and placed under the head of the unfortunate sufferer.

As is usual in such circumstances, one of my first actions was to lift the eyelids of the patient. The eyes were turned upward, as one would expect in such a case, but the pupils were contracted, almost to pinpoints. The breathing was rapid and shallow and the pulse fluttered in a peculiar fashion. "I am correct in assuming that he did not appear in a state of intoxication before his collapse ? " I asked, though it was reasonably certain that his symptoms were not caused by alcohol.

"No, sir," replied one of the fisherman. "I'll take my oath he was stone cold sober when he walked in here."

"Though he looked a little queer, like," added another.

"In what way ? " I asked.

"Well, I'd have to say he looked happy, and cheerful, without there being anything really for him to be happy about. I asked him what was up, and he said 'Nothing', so I left it at that, sir. It's not like he was staggering around or anything like that."

I added "irrational euphoria" to my mental list of the patient's symptoms, and then asked, "What happened next ? "

"Well, sir, he ordered his beer—that's it that you see in front of him on the table right now, and b— me if he didn't just fall down of a heap on the floor. So we picked him up and we put him there, and Davy there was going to call for the doctor. But then Jim Stott," he pointed to the land-lord, "reminded us that Doctor Pengelly had made his way over to St. Mawes and probably wouldn't be back until lat-er this afternoon. Then someone remembered that Elsie Buncombe had some gentlemen from London staying with her, with one of them being a doctor, that one being your-self, sir."

"I see. Thank you. Does anyone know what he was do-ing before he entered this place ? "

Another of the fishermen spoke up. "I saw him earlier this morning, working in the garden at Sir Roderick's."

"That would be who ? " I asked the landlord.

"Sir Roderick Gilbert-Pryor, sir," he replied.

"The Cabinet Minister ? " I asked.

"That's the one, sir. He owns the big house up the way."

"I see. Well, based on my examination of the patient, I would surmise that he is in no immediate danger. However, I think at this moment it would be best if he were not moved from here. I am afraid, landlord, that you will have to accommodate your guest here for a few hours longer. If you have a blanket to throw over him, that would be advis-able, and a hot-water bottle for his feet would be a welcome touch." I pulled out my watch. "If he has not returned to consciousness by half-past four, have no hesitation in call-ing on me again."

"Much obliged, I am sure," said the landlord, passing the word for the blanket and hot-water bottle. "May I recom-mend a pint of the local ale, sir ? On the house, naturally, in gratitude for your help just now."

"With pleasure," I assured him, and raised the foaming tankard. "Your good health, landlord. And good health to all in this room," raising my glass pointedly towards the prone figure on the settle.

RETURNED to our lodgings after this little episode to discover Holmes waiting for me in our drawing-room. I gave him an explanation of where I had been, and he questioned me minutely regarding the symptoms of the sufferer.

"I am surprised, Watson," he exclaimed, when I had finished recounting the event, "that you failed to recognize the symptoms of opiate poisoning."

I smote my brow. "Of course ! I do not know how I came to overlook it."

"In the same way that most such occurrences are overlooked," said Holmes calmly.

"Explain yourself." I was still smarting from the rebuke he had administered to my professional ability, and I spoke somewhat curtly.

"It is a mere matter of association. Who, for example, would ever suspect the presence of typhoid fever, a disease linked to dirt and inadequate sanitation, in a palace ? And yet, I assure you, such cases occur. Or, for that matter, gout, which is commonly linked to wealthy port-drinking elderly men, in the young daughter of a farm labourer ? And yet, as you well know, there are such cases. Opium, no doubt, is something you associate with India and China and if you conceive of it in this country, it is in connection with fashionable ladies or poets in the form of laudanum – maybe with our urban poor. But to think of opium in conjunction with these hearty fisher lads is inconceivable, is it not ? "

I nodded mutely, convinced of the justice of his words.

"If I ever achieve any small measure of success in my cases," he went on, "it is because I am prepared to conceive the inconceivable, and to accept it as a possibility. I am convinced that the same truth applies to other fields, such as the one of medicine."

I silently swallowed my pride and agreed with him.

"But never fear, Watson," he added. "You have done me a great service in this way. In any case, from what you have described, the patient was in no real danger, and your reputation as a doctor will suffer no injury."

At that moment, there was a knock on the door. "It's Jim Stott's boy to see you, Doctor."

"Show him in."

The urchin, cap in hand, stood in the doorway. "Father sends his compliments, and says to tell you that Harry's now feeling much better and sitting up and talking and such."

I smiled. "Tell your father to give Harry plenty of water to drink, and tell Harry from me not to be so foolish in the future. Do you understand ? "

"Yes, sir," said the boy. I tossed him a few coppers, which he caught neatly, and he ran off, closing the door behind him.

"I have done you a great service ? How is that ? " I asked Holmes, baffled by his earlier words.

"Watson, I must confess to you that we are not in this town merely on account of a whim of mine. I had a very definite purpose in mind when I proposed coming here. I admit that the prospect is pleasant, the air refreshing, and Mrs. Buncombe a most congenial landlady, but this was not my principal aim."

"What, then ? "

"Where was your unfortunate patient working before he was stricken, did you say ? "

"In the garden of Sir Roderick Gilbert-Pryor," I replied. "The Cabinet Minister."

"I have had my eye on Sir Roderick for some time," replied Holmes. "He is not, I believe, a rich man. His estates in this part of the world scarcely extend past his immediate neighbourhood. Much was mortgaged and subsequently disposed of by his late father, who seems to have speculated unwisely in railway shares. Sir Roderick holds a few directorships in the City, which presumably bring in a little income, but other than that, he would seem to have little money, and yet he manages to entertain on a lavish scale and maintain his position on a level more than consistent with his Ministerial rank."

"His wife's money ? " I proposed.

"There is none. Lady Jocelyn is the youngest daughter of a country parson. It was a love match, and was certainly not contracted for money on his side. Nor hers, I am sure. Whatever the list of sins that Sir Roderick may have committed, fortune hunting would not appear to be included in it."

"You mean that we came here for the sole purpose of examining the state of Sir Roderick Gilbert-Pryor's finances ? " I asked, somewhat incredulously. "Why could not this have been achieved from London ? "

"I have already done all I could in this regard as far as London is concerned," Holmes answered. "I felt it was time to investigate the matter from here."

"You continue to amaze me, Holmes. May I ask why you are doing this ? "

"It is at the request of the Prime Minister," he replied. "He, too, has noticed the discrepancy between Sir Roderick's income and his expenditure. He fears the possibility of an associated scandal, and he wishes to prevent the occurrence of any such. He has therefore retained me to make such enquiries as are necessary."

I could not refrain from bursting out laughing. "So you and I are here at the orders of the British Government ! " I exclaimed. "And what conclusions have you reached so far ? "

"None that makes any sense," he admitted. "The business I uncovered this morning distracted me a little, I admit, but may well be connected with my original object in coming here, now I come to reflect on the matter. The business you have just attended to makes me believe that there is something more in this place that I can use to provide my explanations to the Prime Minister, however."

I considered what Holmes had just said. " This is mere supposition on my part," I admitted, "but what if the operations of which we discovered the traces this morning, whatever they turn out to be, are definitely connected with Sir Roderick ? "

" I think this connection to be most likely," remarked Holmes, "but without any further detailed knowledge of these operations, we are no further forward in our enquiries, and it is fruitless to speculate on the matter. By the by, Mrs. Buncombe's expression last night after dinner when I lit my pipe leads me to believe she is no lover of tobacco indoors. I will therefore take my pipe and ponder these matters in the garden."

I was left alone in the room, and decided to study the latest edition of the *Lancet*, which I had brought down from London with me. By a strange coincidence, one of the articles dealt with a new drug, based on opium, and developed in Germany. The drug, diacetylmorphine, was being marketed in Germany for the purpose of suppressing coughs under the name of "Heroin", and was claimed by the makers to eliminate the unfortunate dependency, amounting almost to addiction, to which users of morphine were prone. I marked the article, and determined to show it to Holmes when he arrived from the garden. The rest of the journal was of less immediate interest, but I noted the name of one of my former fellow-students at Barts, who seemed to be making a name for himself in a specialised field of surgery.

When Holmes returned from the garden, I showed the article to him. He read it through, with particular attention to the process described therein for the manufacture of the drug.

" I have heard of this opiate," he told me, "but this is the most detailed and trustworthy information I have come across so far. You are to be congratulated on drawing it to my attention. Would you say that the symptoms you observed earlier today corresponded to the description here of a patient who has inadvertently taken too much of the drug ? ”

“Certainly, but they could apply to any of the opiates, as you are yourself aware.”

“Nonetheless, Watson,” and Holmes turned to me, his eyes glittering, “I believe we are about to discover the mysterious source of Sir Roderick's wealth.”

“Sir Roderick is not engaged in the pharmaceutical trade, is he ? ” I asked.

“He holds a directorship in one of the smaller pharmaceutical companies,” replied my friend, “and his name is not unknown among amateur practitioners of the chemical sciences. The production of this 'Heroin' would not be beyond his powers, nor would the procurement of the necessary apparatus pose any problem.”

“But surely,” I retorted, “even if he were producing this drug, it would be for the good of mankind.”

“Ah, Watson, you know only what you read here,” pointing to the *Lancet*. “My sources tell me that far from reducing the dependency which makes morphine so undesirable to many, this drug turns its user into a virtual slave, whose animal craving produces physical and mental horrors beyond all imagination. Furthermore, the effects of the drug when it is first administered are reportedly of an ecstasy beyond compare. I thank you for assisting me to end my dependence on cocaine, but I confess that the pleasure that I obtained from that drug in my idle hours was indeed as exquisite as the pain it cost me to break the habit. If this 'Heroin' is more powerful in each regard…”

“I know what it cost you to break that habit,” I replied, “and I salute your courage in having done so.”

“What,” Holmes continued, ignoring me, “if some unscrupulous fiend were to dose others with this new drug, knowing that they would become, as it were, hooked on it like fish on a line, and would demand more of it, paying any price to obtain their ration ? ”

I shuddered. "That would indeed be inhuman," I agreed. "And you believe Sir Roderick Gilbert-Pryor, a Minister of the Crown, is engaged in such a vile trade ? "

"I now have reason to suspect so," replied my friend gravely. "Tomorrow, we will attempt to ascertain the truth. If Sir Roderick turns out to have a missing right incisor, I will know that my suspicions are correct."

"And if they are ? "

My friend shrugged. "That is not for me to decide. I make my report to Downing-street, and the matter is then out of my hands. But come, my nose informs me of a roast fowl, and if Mrs. Buncombe's skills tonight match those of last night, we shall be well fed indeed."

HE next morning arrived, thankfully without revolver practice, and Holmes and I settled down to a breakfast consisting chiefly of a fine *kitchari* which brought back memories of my service in India.

"Today, we visit Sir Roderick," proclaimed Holmes.

"And if he is not at home ? "

"He will not be in London, during the Parliamentary recess," Holmes pointed out. "This is his only country place, and I think it more than likely that he will be here. It wants three weeks until the Glorious Twelfth, so he will not be on the grouse moors. It is conceivable, I suppose, that he may be staying with a colleague in Scotland, tormenting salmon with those ridiculous artificial flies, but the odds are against it."

"I have never understood your prejudice against angling, Holmes, but let that pass. Let us assume, then, that Sir Roderick will be at home. On what grounds do you propose to make his acquaintance ? "

"We are already acquainted," replied Holmes. "I believe I mentioned last night that he is an amateur chemist of some considerable ability. I, too, have dabbled in the subject, as you know, and he and I once collaborated on a work dealing with the use of acetone as a universal solvent. We have encountered each other with relative frequency over the past few years at meetings of the Chemical Society and the like. On the last occasion we met, some twelve months ago, he apparently was in possession of all his teeth, as I recall, but one never knows what accidents may have befallen him in that line since that time."

We enquired the way to Sir Roderick's of Mrs. Buncombe, and set off on what she assured us was an easy walk. Along the way, Holmes, to my surprise, purchased a bag of small green apples.

"These look nourishing enough," he remarked, in answer to my questioning glance.

"They hardly appeared to be the most appetising specimens on display," I objected.

"They will serve their purpose," he replied, enigmatically.

On arrival at Sir Roderick's establishment, a fine example of the architecture of the last century, but one which had been allowed to fall into decay, Holmes' conjecture was proved to be correct. A servant took our cards, and returned to inform us that Sir Roderick was at home and would receive us. We were conducted to a handsome room that appeared to serve as both a library and as Sir Roderick's study.

The Minister rose from behind his desk to greet us.

"Holmes," he exclaimed, smiling widely, showing us a perfect row of even white teeth, somewhat, I confess, to my disappointment. "How good to see you here. If you'd let me know before you arrived, I would have been delighted to offer you my hospitality. Your assistance would be invaluable with one or two little problems I am currently encountering in my laboratory. I would be more than happy to have you and your friend here as my guests."

Holmes bowed as he introduced me, and I bowed to the baronet in my turn. "You give my poor efforts far too much praise," remarked Holmes. "We are very comfortably lodged in one of the houses of the town, and we would not dream of imposing on your generous nature."

It may have been my fancy, but it seemed to me that a look of relief seemed to pass over Sir Roderick's face as Holmes declined the invitation. "Very well, as you will," he said, "but I must insist on your dining with me some night. Let me see now," he went on, consulting a notebook, "tonight I am engaged, and the next night as well, but maybe the day after that ? Good. I shall expect you about seven, then. And since we are in the country, I feel there is no need to dress. Pray feel free to make yourself as comfortable as you please in these rural surroundings." He could not have been more affable, but I felt that some of his sociability was a little forced, and this was confirmed in his answer to Holmes' next enquiry, about Lady Jocelyn.

"The poor gal is not in the best of health these days, I am sorry to say. She came down from London three months ago, and has hardly left her room since that time. The local doctor, Dr. Pengelly, is an excellent man, and we have also had specialists from London come to examine her, but their efforts to discover the cause of her indisposition have so far remained fruitless."

I forbore from further enquiry, though my professional interest was naturally piqued, but felt it was hardly my place to interfere, and I doubted my ability to be of any practical value in the case, particularly if the finest doctors in the land had declared themselves baffled.

"I am sorry to hear that," replied Holmes. "Please present my regards to her."

"I will certainly do that," replied Sir Roderick. "What, if I may be so bold as to ask, do you have there, by the way ? I am intrigued." He gestured towards the bag of apples that Holmes still carried in his hand.

"Some local agricultural specimens," replied my friend, "which I purchased on a sudden impulse on my way here.

Perhaps you would care for one ? " So saying, he pressed one into my hand before offering the bag to Sir Roderick, who looked at him in some perplexity.

" Well, this is most kind of you," said Sir Roderick, selecting an apple for himself, and polishing it on a handkerchief that he withdrew from his sleeve. He inspected the apple with a critical eye. " I hope you are not offended, Holmes, but I will reserve this for my dessert following luncheon. My digestion, you know."

" Naturally," Holmes replied. In the meantime, I had taken a bite of the fruit that Holmes had forced on me, and discovered it to be as hard and sour as I had surmised from its appearance. I stealthily placed the remainder into my coat pocket, without, I hoped, either of the others becoming aware of my having done so. Holmes, I noticed, was not partaking of his purchase.

After a little conversation between the other two concerning chemical subjects, which, to be frank, was of no interest to me and beyond my powers of comprehension, and a renewed invitation to and acceptance of dinner on the day after the next, we took our leave of Sir Roderick.

" My dear fellow," I said to Holmes, as we were walking down the drive of Sir Roderick's house, through the spacious gardens. " Why on earth did you give me one of those damnable apples ? "

He ignored my words, but fixed his attention on the flower-beds on each side of the path. " Look here, Watson. What do you see ? "

I answered rather sharply, I am afraid. The memory of the apple was still with me, and I feared I had loosened one of my back teeth when biting it. " Poppies, of course."

" Of course," he said. " You were in Afghanistan, were you not ? "

" You know well that I served there in my Army days. I fail to see the point of the question."

" Afghanistan grows a certain type of poppy, as I am sure

you are aware," he remarked, in a conversational tone.

"So it does. The opium poppy." I stopped and looked more closely at the flowers beside me. "By Jove, Holmes ! And in plain sight of all ! Whoever would have suspected a Minister of the Crown to be cultivating such a thing ? "

" I remarked to you yesterday on the principles of association and incongruity. Consider this to be another example of the same."

"Remarkable," I said.

"Not so remarkable, I feel." We passed through the gates, and Holmes held out his hand to me, in which lay a few long serrated leaves of some plant, arranged themselves somewhat like the outstretched fingers of a hand. "Do you recognise this ? "

I looked closely. "*Cannabis sativa,*" I replied. "Another herb, producing fibres used in the production of rope."

"It is also held to produce some sort of effect on those who eat it or smoke it," added Holmes. "I plucked this from Sir Roderick's garden just now. However, this plant is growing rampant throughout the vicinity. I noticed many such examples as we walked from the station the other day. It appears to be a positive weed in this town. Its use must be quite common here."

I considered the other more usual employment of this plant. "This is a port," I remarked to Holmes, "and the ships and boats require hempen rigging. There is nothing more natural that the boatmen here would have cultivated the plant locally for this purpose before the advent of modern transportation permitted the ropes to be brought from a central manufactory."

"Quite possibly you are correct," replied Holmes. "But it is an indubitable fact that the distinctive aroma of the smoke of this herb was to be perceived just now while we were talking to Sir Roderick."

" He is under the influence of this drug ? "

" Maybe not he. Maybe his wife, or conceivably one of the

servants. His wife's being ill may or may not be another suspicious circumstance. Unless I am aware of the nature of Lady Jocelyn's complaint, I cannot be sure. But there are many little factors here, Watson, none of them of great importance in themselves, but added together—"

I stopped suddenly in my tracks, and gave a small cry.

" What is the matter ? " my companion asked me.

" My tooth," I complained bitterly. " Your damned apple." I clutched the side of my face. " I feel I must seek the service of a dentist immediately."

" Dear, dear," said Holmes in an animated fashion. " How very fortunate."

" ' Fortunate', did you say, Holmes ? I am in some pain, I assure you." I was almost angry with my friend.

" Did I indeed say ' fortunate' ? I meant ' unfortunate', naturally," he replied. For a moment I almost believed I had misheard his previous utterance, such was his sympathetic tone.

We enquired of a passer-by regarding the existence of a dentist in the town, and were informed that there was one such, whose services were highly praised by our informant.

" I will wait in the waiting-room while your tooth is attended to," said Holmes to me as we entered the dental surgery. " I trust that there will not be anything seriously amiss."

The dentist, a Mr. Garland, indeed proved to be splendidly competent. Anointing the afflicted sub-molar with oil of cloves, he advised me to avoid using that side of my mouth for mastication for a few days, and invited me to visit him again should the pain continue after that time.

I emerged from the surgery to the waiting room to discover Holmes lounging there, seemingly engrossed in a copy of the *Illustrated London News*.

" Nothing serious, I trust ? " he asked with an expression of great concern. There seemed to be, however, a sense of triumph in his voice, the reason for which I was totally at a loss to discover.

"No thanks to you," I grudgingly replied.

"I apologise, Watson," he answered me. "Fully and without reserve. I hereby dispose of the offending articles. They have served their purpose – indeed, better than I expected them to do." So saying, he dropped the apples, still in their bag, into a small stream that flowed beside the road along which we were walking. In a slightly better mood than previously, I retrieved the half-apple from my pocket, and sent it flying to join its fellows.

"Our next port of call is the post-office," went on Holmes. "We must act fast, I fear."

At the post-office, Holmes wrote out a telegram to London, which he dispatched reply-paid.

"And now to Mrs. Buncombe's, to await the reply, which should be with us in an hour or less, if luck is with us."

It proved to be about an hour and a half before Holmes received his reply. "Excellent, Watson ! " was his comment upon reading it. "Now let us have a few words with our worthy hostess."

"Mrs. Buncombe," he enquired of her a few minutes later, "two friends of mine will be arriving in this town later today. Would it be possible for them to take lodging with you, at the same rates as Dr. Watson and myself for one, possibly two nights, from tonight ? "

"With pleasure, sir, though you must admit it is somewhat short notice," she smiled. "These would be gentlemen, I take it ? "

"Two Chinese gentlemen," replied Holmes. Her face changed slightly as she digested the news. "One of them is a product of Oxford University, and a credit to our civilisation and his. As to the other, I confess I do not know well, but I am fully prepared to take full responsibility for him. Naturally, I will pay you in advance for their lodging," he added, withdrawing his wallet, and presenting her with a Bank of England note. "This will compensate you for any inconvenience, I think ? "

"Well, if these Chinamen are known to you, sir, I suppose there'll be no trouble in putting them up here. In the usual run of things, of course, I wouldn't dream of such a thing. But seeing as you are being so generous about these matters, sir, I have to say I will be happy to fall in with your wishes. I'll put them up in the back. I take it they won't take it amiss if they share a room ? "

"Capital ! " he answered her. "Thank you, Mrs. Buncombe. I will leave all the domestic arrangements to your good sense. Now, Watson," he addressed me, as she left the room, "we have work to do, and only a little time to do it in. Tonight, after dinner, we will make another little expedition to the castle."

"Why tonight ? " I asked.

"Because, my dear fellow, Sir Roderick informed us that tonight and tomorrow night he would be unable to dine with us. I scarcely think that the social whirl of this charming little backwater is of such intensity that he is engaged for those evenings—at least not in the conventional sense. Furthermore, I would draw your attention to the calendar."

"What of it ? "

"Tonight and tomorrow are nights of the new moon."

"I begin to perceive your meaning."

"So let us look out some dark clothing, in which we may not easily be observed, and do you, Watson, procure a pair of dark lanterns for us. I venture to suggest that a stout walking stick might also be of use in the coming days."

"And you ? "

"I must go to the harbour, where I will make arrangements for tomorrow."

OLMES' two mysterious Chinamen arrived by train late in the afternoon. One was a smaller, slightly corpulent, man of about the same age as Holmes and myself, who wore Western clothes in impeccable taste. He extended his hand to me as Holmes introduced us.

"John Chen. Delighted to meet the Boswell of the great detective at last," he announced, in English that was the equal of any gentleman's of this land.

The other Chinaman was of a very different character. He was tall where the other was short, and slender, almost to the point of emaciation, where the other was plump. He was dressed in a loose-fitting dark costume of vaguely Oriental cut, and carried on his back a large wicker basket, out of which came strange cheeping noises, accompanied by a strong smell strongly redolent of fish that was not quite fresh.

"This is Wang Lee," explained Chen. "He speaks little English, but he is utterly reliable, I assure you."

The taller Chinaman turned to Holmes and myself, and bowed to us, his hands clasped together and tucked into his voluminous sleeves. "Happy to meet you," he said in heavy accents.

"Let us go," said Holmes. "You will be sleeping tonight at the house of our landlady, Mrs. Buncombe, who will be providing us with food. I trust that Wang Lee can stomach our European food ? "

Chen turned to the other, and spoke to him in their curious sing-song language, receiving a reply in the same tongue.

"He says that European food is not to his taste, but for one or two days, he can stomach it, given the fee you will be paying him."

"Good," said Holmes. We had arrived at our lodgings. "I hardly think that this will be welcome indoors," he said, indicating Wang Lee's basket. "There is a tool-shed at the rear that may be suitable for it. I do not think we need trouble asking Mrs. Buncombe's permission to use the facility for one night only." He led the way, and the basket was placed within the shed.

"You have fish ? " Wang Lee addressed me directly.

"What does he mean ? " I asked of his compatriot.

"Ah yes, of course." Holmes, rather than Chen, answered me. "It is natural to assume that some fish will be required. Watson, I realise it is an imposition on your good nature, but if you would make your way to the fishing port and purchase some dozen of small fish – pilchards or the like, and as fresh as you can obtain them – I am sure that Mr. Lee and his charge would be more than grateful. While you are gone, I will take the opportunity of outlining the situation to our friends."

I was puzzled, to say the least, but Holmes' mysterious commands often failed to make sense at the time, revealing their purpose only later, so I hastened to carry out this strange errand. I returned some twenty minutes later with a paper package suspended at a safe distance from my hand by a loop of string. In truth, the smell of the fish was nowhere near as strong as I had feared.

I returned, and viewed the three men in conference, still standing outside the tool-shed. I presented the package to Wang Lee, who opened it with obvious signs of satisfaction, and disappeared with it into the shed. Loud squawking sounds and other noises came from the shed, which ceased as Wang Lee emerged again.

"All finish," he beamed happily.

"Excellent," replied Holmes. "Then let us go inside."

Mrs. Buncombe rose to the challenge of her Oriental visitors, and greeted them with what appeared to be unfeigned pleasure. Chen won her heart by praising her collection of Oriental knick-knacks brought from the East by her late husband, and Wang Lee sat impassively silent, doing nothing that might cause any offence.

The meal was very much to my taste, consisting chiefly of a roast of pork loin, and if it was not to Wang Lee's, he disguised his feelings well.

After dinner, the two Chinamen retired to their room, and Holmes and I to ours, where we changed our garments and prepared for the evening to come.

"I have already informed Mrs. Buncombe that we will be out late tonight," Holmes informed me as we left the house, "and she has kindly lent me the latchkey."

"What reason did you assign for our absence ? "

"Why, none. She never enquired, and I did not see fit to tell her."

"Holmes, I must ask you this. What are we looking for tonight, and why are those Chinamen staying with us ? "

"As to the first, I am not as yet certain, and as to the second, I propose that you see with your own eyes tomorrow morning."

After a short walk, we reached the castle, and positioned ourselves where we could enjoy a clear view of the lighthouse.

It was, despite the time of year, a somewhat cool evening, and I was beginning to wish that I had packed my hipflask, which contained some excellent brandy, when Holmes grasped my arm.

"Look ! " he commanded, pointing towards the lighthouse, which was flashing in its assigned pattern every fifteen seconds.

"I see nothing," I complained.

"There, below the cliff, and above the water. One red light and one green. Do you not see ? "

My eyes followed his pointing finger, and indeed, I could just make out two coloured specks of light in the places indicated. It was, as Holmes had remarked earlier, a night on which there was almost no moon, and I had to strain my eyes to discern the details of any objects surrounding the lights. "I see them, Holmes. Are they the riding lights of fishing boats ? "

He shook his head. "No, they are not moving. These

are fixed lights. Here," and he passed me a pair of powerful field-glasses, which showed me that that the lights appeared to come from lanterns affixed to poles in the water, the support of the red lantern being taller than that of the green. "With a little mental agility on our part," went on Holmes, "I think we are able to ascertain their purpose."

"Your meaning ? "

"Imagine yourself in a position so that the lights are in line with each other, the red above the green. Where does that lead ? "

I pondered the conundrum which, as Holmes had remarked, required not a little mental effort. "It leads to the cove behind Mrs. Buncombe's house. And these lights therefore serve as a guide to the visitors who come and leave the beer bottles."

"Indeed so, Watson. And look ! " his finger pointed to a barely discernible shape in the water which I recognised, with the aid of the field-glasses, as being a small sailing vessel, scarcely more than a dinghy. "And another ! "

"We should summon the police," I told Holmes.

He shook his head in reply. "This is no matter for the police. Remember, the whole purpose of my investigation is to prevent a possible scandal, not to cause one," he reminded me. "I am confident we will have our chance to nip this business in the bud tomorrow night. For now, let us content ourselves with being observers, and tomorrow morning, my plan is to discover still more." He rubbed his hands together in anticipation.

I quite forgot the chill of the evening as we spent the next hour observing about a dozen small boats make their way to the hidden cove. Most appeared to come from the open sea, but there was one notable exception – a pleasure yacht by her appearance, which made its way from the general quarter of the lighthouse, starting out some ten minutes after the last small boat had entered the cove. "I had guessed as much," remarked Holmes, when I pointed out this vessel to him. After this yacht had reached the cove, the two guiding lights were extinguished, and we could see no movement for about another hour. I was once again regretting my lack of foresight in the matter of my hip-flask, and was about to propose to Holmes that we quit the place, when he drew my attention to a procession of small boats leaving the cove. "The evening's entertainment is at an end," he said softly to me. "We may withdraw now, I think."

Confident that my friend had solved at least part of the riddle, I thankfully turned my steps towards Mrs. Buncombe's house, and the warmth of my bed.

HE next morning saw Holmes and myself at breakfast. We were joined halfway through our repast by John Chen, who bade us a good morning and tucked into his porridge, followed by bacon and eggs, like any Englishman. Indeed, were it not for his physiognomy, and basing one's judgement only on his speech and dress, one would have taken him for a native of these shores.

"Wang Lee is upstairs, but will join us when we are ready," he explained, helping himself to toast and marmalade.

"Watson," remarked Holmes to me as we left Chen finishing the last of his coffee. "We will be spending a day on the water. The field-glasses, and dare I suggest it, your hip-flask, would be of great utility, I think. I would also advise warm clothing."

Soon after, he and I, accompanied by the two Chinamen, with Wang Lee carrying the mysterious basket with which he had arrived, made our way to the harbour, where two small rowing boats awaited us, presumably the results of Holmes' visit the previous day.

Holmes greeted the boatmen standing by, and proceeded to commandeer one of the boats for himself and me, leaving the other to be occupied by the two Orientals. John Chen, dressed in a smart blue duffel-coat, manned the oars, with Wang Lee, now in bright unmistakably Chinese garb, and his mysterious basket occupying the bow. Holmes took the oars of our craft.

"I may require you to provide our propulsive power at some future point in our expedition," he remarked to me, "but at present I will indulge myself in a little exercise." I have mentioned in the past that Holmes, though of what appeared to be a thin sinewy build, was possessed of considerable strength which was in no way hinted at by his appearance. He proved himself to be an oarsman of no mean skill, and we were soon in the middle of the channel separating the port from the lighthouse. "You may care to observe that post that we are about to pass," said Holmes.

The post to which he referred was a wooden pole, protruding from the surface of the water for about ten feet. Affixed to the top of the pole was a hook.

"Undoubtedly," I remarked, "this hook was used to attach one of the lanterns that we saw last night."

"I am convinced of it," replied Holmes. "If you will take the trouble to look in the other direction towards our lodgings on the other side of the channel, you will see the other pole to which the green lantern was attached."

I looked in the direction indicated, and indeed, the two poles pointed straight toward the hidden cove at the bottom of the orchard.

"I think there can be little doubt," added Holmes, "of the purpose of these poles, which are clearly placed here as a support for the lanterns that we observed last night. It is plain that they have been placed as navigation aids to guide visitors to this secret landing place."

We rowed on a little further, taking careful note of the position of the poles and their relationship to the lighthouse.

"I think," Holmes remarked, "we were best if we moved to one side of here," and so saying, pulled us closer to the coast, along the shore from the lighthouse, but in a position from where we were still able to observe it.

"What is our plan ? " I asked Holmes.

"We attempt to catch some mackerel," replied, bringing out a couple of hand-lines from under the thwart on which he was sitting, much to my amusement, given his past remarks about anglers. "And while we are doing this, we will watch the reactions of those in there," glancing towards the lighthouse, "to the antics of my friends there," glancing towards the boat containing the two Chinese. "By the by, Watson, I would advise you to pull that cap of yours a little further forward over your eyes. Your face is too visible for my liking."

"I had no idea my appearance offended you to that extent," I retorted.

Holmes chuckled. "My dear fellow, this concerns the matter of your possible identification by person or persons unknown from there," looking once more towards the lighthouse, "and has little to do with my pleasure or otherwise concerning the sight of your countenance."

"What in the world are they doing ? " I asked, looking at the other boat, as we cast the fishing lines over the side of the boat. Wang Lee had opened the basket, out of which appeared a large black bird with a long neck.

"That, my dear fellow, is probably the only example of its kind in the British Isles. It is a cormorant, as you have probably deduced for yourself, but one which has been trained to catch fish and return them to its master. Wang Lee is probably the sole practitioner of the skill in this country, and we are lucky that he is a friend of John Chen who was able to persuade him to help us in this way."

"How do you come to know Chen ? "

"I would have thought it evident. We were fellow students at University. His father is some kind of nobleman in his own country, and he wished one of his sons to learn more about the Western barbarians, as we appear to that ancient civilisation. Chan and I have maintained contact since our student days, and he has been of invaluable assistance to me whenever I have wished to know more about anything concerning the land of Cathay or its inhabitants."

As I watched, the bird dived off the edge of the boat, and disappeared beneath the waves. Some twenty seconds later, the sleek black head broke the surface of the water, a fish of some six inches in length held in its beak.

"Holmes, I appreciate that this Oriental and his bird possess a certain skill, but what is the purpose here ? "

"It is a bow drawn at a venture, I confess, but one that may well prove to be of great value," replied Holmes. "It is a curious sight to watch, is it not ? " I assented. Indeed, my eyes were fixed on the interplay between man and bird, as the latter continued to dive and retrieve silver fish from the depths. Every few attempts, Wang Lee would reward the creature for its efforts by allowing it to devour one of its catch. "My hope is," went on Holmes, "that the inhabitants of the lighthouse will likewise find this an intriguing sight and will show themselves on this balcony the better to observe these strange goings-on. And here," he said, "is the first of them."

A figure had indeed appeared on the balcony, and was watching the antics of the Chinese and the bird with rapt attention. Holmes took the field-glasses and, as surreptitiously as he could manage, watched the other through them. He shook his head. "Not yet, I fear, but there is still time."

He gave no indication of the meaning of his last words, and started to whistle idly, in defiance of the popular superstition among sailors governing the practice. "Aha ! " he suddenly exclaimed. "This is what I have been waiting for ! "

The man on the balcony had obviously been calling to another within the building, though his words were inaudible to us at our distance. It appeared that his call had been answered and he was joined on the balcony by another figure, seemingly clad in a curious white garment.

"We have him ! " exclaimed Holmes, peering through the field-glasses and handing them to me. "You are my witness to this, Watson. Tell me what you see."

I adjusted the focus. "It is Sir Roderick," I replied. "And he appears to be wearing a laboratory coat."

"Precisely so," replied Holmes. "This is not evidence that can stand up in a court of law, naturally, but it is further evidence for my case, even so."

"Evidence of what, Holmes ? "

"Evidence, naturally, that the lighthouse is being used as a laboratory for the production of this 'Heroin', and that Sir Roderick himself is the principal agent in its production. We have seen enough, Watson. It is now time for us to return. May I trouble you to take the oars this time ? I wish to consider our next move." With that, he relinquished control of the boat to me, and curled up in the bow, the smoke from his pipe making us appear from a distance to be more of a steam-launch than a simple rowing boat.

HAT evening, John Chen and Wang Lee having departed Falmouth, together with the cormorant and a suitable supply of fish, which included several fine mackerel caught by Holmes and myself in the course of our surveillance, we prepared for our nocturnal expedition.

"I do not anticipate immediate violence from the principal in this affair," Holmes said to me. "It would be the height of folly for Sir Roderick to attempt any such moves, particularly as we are both known in the neighbourhood, following your recent medical ministrations in the public house. His minions, on the other hand, may prove a trifle less amenable to reason, and so I am taking my revolver as an additional inducement, should my words prove ineffective in this regard. You could do worse than to equip yourself with that ashplant you purchased yesterday."

His words seemed to me to be practical, and I therefore picked up the stout stick, testing its balance, and hoping that I would not have occasion to use it in the fashion that Holmes had just described.

"Tonight, tempting as it may be, I fear that your hip-flask must be left behind, Watson. We must be silent as the grave."

"I trust that will not prove to be a prophetic simile," I remarked.

"Do not fear," said Holmes. "As I say, I am relatively confident that there will be no physical violence on this occasion, but even so, I feel it will be as well for us both to be prepared against such a possibility. Have you the dark lanterns ? Excellent. Let us sally forth, and prepare to meet the foe. I have already marked out a spot where we can wait undetected until the time is ripe."

Dressed in our dark garments, and with black cloths tied about our faces, we must have been nearly invisible from only a few yards away. On this moonless night, though Holmes was a matter of feet away from me as we moved through the orchard, I nonetheless lost sight of him on more than one occasion, and was only able to track his progress from the faint sounds that he made. I had confidence that, with Holmes having displayed his usual sagacity in the matter of concealment, there was little or no danger of our discovery.

On this occasion, since we had a good expectation in our minds of what was about to transpire, the period of waiting did not seem to be so long, as we strained our eyes for the glimmer of light that would show us that the evening's business was about to begin.

After what I judged to be about an hour, Holmes grasped my arm, "Do you see that, Watson ? " The green light had appeared as a faint glow in the distance toward the light-house. "The game is about to commence." Even though Holmes spoke in a low whisper, his obvious excitement at the events about to unfold before us was almost palpable. After a few minutes, the red light also made its appearance. As we had surmised earlier, the two lights were almost in line with the lighthouse from our position at the side of the cove.

It was a matter of a few minutes only before the first boat appeared. " I cannot be certain of this," Holmes whispered to me, " but I would wager that this is a local party from this vicinity. The boats from the other villages round about will be along shortly, I am sure."

He was proved correct in his surmise. Over the next twenty minutes, about ten boats appeared and beached themselves on the sandy shore of the cove. None of these was a large boat, and each was crewed by two, or at the most three, men, who joined together in a group which as yet lacked a focus. Obviously, they were waiting for the yacht that we had observed last night to come from the lighthouse. As we watched, one of them lit a lantern, and swing it over his head, waving it three times slowly from left to right. From the base of the lighthouse, we saw a similar moving light.

" Those signals and acknowledgement are to let him know they are all waiting, and there is no danger ? " I whispered to Holmes.

" I am certain of it," he hissed in return.

Holmes continued to peer through the field glasses that we had brought with us, and I suddenly felt him quiver with excitement.

" It is he ! I am sure of it ! " he whispered to me. " Now we have him, I am positive."

In a few minutes, even without the aid of the field glasses, I was able to discern the dark shape of the yacht making its way from the lighthouse towards us. A few minutes more, and we heard the sound of the boat's dinghy being launched and the regular splashes of its oars as it was rowed towards us.

Holmes put his lips to my ear. "On my signal," he said in a low voice, "we will rush into the middle with our lanterns fully open. Attempt to hold your lantern in such a way that the light will dazzle the others without yourself being so inconvenienced. Though I have remarked, I do not expect violence, be alert for any mischief that may occur."

The two leading lights had now gone out, and the visitors from the yacht stepped out of the small rowing boat, now beached on the shore. Even in the dim light, it was possible to recognise the tall powerful figure of Sir Roderick. I guessed that Holmes would be experiencing a feeling of inner satisfaction that his deductions of the previous days had now finally proven themselves to be correct.

"Now, Watson, now ! " he hissed at me, and sprang from our hiding place, uttering an unearthly scream of a peculiar calibre, the like of which I had never heard him utter in the past, and which froze the blood in my veins. To me, who knew the source of the sound, it was frightening. To the waiting men, who had no idea of where this uncanny sound was coming, it must have seemed almost supernatural. The effect was to make them freeze and stop in their tracks as if they had been turned to stone by some monster or basilisk.

"Do not move, or I fire ! " he cried, brandishing his revolver, which was clearly visible in the light of the lantern that he carried in his other hand. I followed Holmes, my lantern held high, with my stout stick in my other hand.

Sir Roderick, for it was indeed he, turned to face Holmes, his face contorted in fury.

"What the devil do you mean by this, Holmes ? " he shouted.

"I might well ask you the same, Sir Roderick," replied Holmes calmly. His quiet tone of voice was in complete contrast to the terrifying bloodcurdling scream that he had uttered just a few seconds before.

The Cabinet Minister drew himself up to his not inconsiderable height. "I think you forget my position, Mr.

Holmes," he replied. His voice was now as calm as that of my friend, but with an unmistakeable undertone of menace. " I am in a position to make your existence more than a trifle uncomfortable in the future, and indeed, I could make it certain that you would never be able to exercise your pernicious arts in this country ever again."

" I think not, Sir Roderick," replied Holmes. " You hardly imagine that I am doing this on my own account, do you ? "

" There is only one man in this kingdom who would have the power to engage you in such a matter," sneered Sir Roderick.

" Indeed that is so," replied Holmes, " and it is he who has engaged me to investigate this affair."

While this exchange had been taking place, I had noticed one of the ruffians from Sir Roderick's boat moving stealthily in Holmes's direction. With horror, I observed that he held a knife in his right hand, with which it appeared he was prepared to attack Holmes. I dashed forward, raising my stick high in the air, and brought it down hard on the wretch's forearm as he was in the instant of striking forward with the blade. There was a loud crack as the bone shattered, and a clatter as the knife dropped to the ground.

Holmes turned briefly in the direction of the sounds and took in the situation at a glance. " My sincere thanks to you, Watson," he remarked. " It would seem that despite Sir Roderick's protestations, some of the gentleman here would have matters that they would sooner keep hidden." He turned to Sir Roderick again. " May I suggest that you dismiss your minions, so that we may continue our conversation more privately ? " he invited.

" Then we can keep the money, sir ? " one of the sailors asked Holmes.

For a few seconds, Holmes appeared to be taken aback. " I think that had better be left with me, don't you ? " he invited, after a few moments' consideration. Sir Roderick watched with what appeared to be mounting fury as the visitors to the cove deposited envelopes and packets at Holmes's feet, but he was powerless to resist with the other's revolver held to his temple, which not only prevented him from resisting our efforts, but also acted as a deterrent to any who might feel inclined to attack either Holmes or myself.

When the last of these packets appeared to have been delivered, Holmes turned to the assembled men. " I suggest that you leave now, and never return. Your services in this area are no longer required." As they departed, he turned to Sir Roderick, whose face was now a mask of rage.

" Do you realise what you have done ? " he fairly screamed at Holmes.

" I have an idea," replied my friend, smiling.

" In a few minutes, you have completely destroyed the work of several years."

" For which the world and especially those poor wretches who you have enslaved to your drug will be profoundly grateful, should they ever discover the truth. I regard your recent actions in this area as being totally despicable, and unworthy of an English gentleman, let alone a Minister of the Crown."

Sir Roderick had the grace to appear somewhat abashed. " What do you propose doing ? " he asked Holmes.

" I am bound to make a report to the Prime Minister," replied Holmes. " Following that, the matter is in his hands, not mine. He will, I am sure, recommend some course of action to you, and I would be extremely surprised if it encompassed your remaining in the Cabinet."

" I am ruined, ruined ! Have you any idea what you have just done ? " he asked again.

For answer, Holmes gestured to me to pick up the envelopes and packets that had been deposited by the boatmen.

" I think it is time to examine the boat in which you arrived," he said to Sir Roderick, after I had retrieved the last of these envelopes. Some were of considerable weight and heft.

Some of the baronet's arrogance and bluster returned to him. "You may search as long and as hard as you please, Mr. Busybody Holmes," he retorted. "I can assure you that even you will find nothing."

Holmes regarded his opponent keenly in the light of the lantern that he shone into the other's face. "I see you are telling the truth," he said at last. "I now perceive that we should have made this expedition last night."

"You are clever, Mr. Holmes," sneered Sir Roderick. "A little too clever for your own good, I would say."

Holmes chose to ignore this, and turned to me. "Come, Watson, our work here is done. Let us to the police station where we are expected," he remarked significantly. "I would not advise following us," he added to Sir Roderick. "Though the local police do not know the reason behind the Home Secretary's personal request to them, I am confident that they will do their duty in ensuring that we come to no harm."

"You will still suffer for this!" fairly screamed Sir Roderick. "I am not without influence in certain areas, and my agents have powers beyond your reckoning."

"I fear that you somewhat underestimate my powers of reckoning," smiled Holmes. "I am well aware of your influence in certain circles, and so, may I add, are various others with whom you and I have mutual acquaintance."

Sir Roderick snarled. There is no other word to describe the animal-like noise that he produced in answer to Holmes's words. "I will see you in hell!"

"We will see about that," Holmes replied. "I expect at least one of us to take up abode in that region at some time in the future."

The other seemed ready to spring on us, but checked himself as Holmes waved his revolver in a significant manner.

"Adieu, Sir Roderick," Holmes called gaily over his shoulder as we left the orchard.

URELY it was obvious from the time that I discovered the beer bottles, even if some of the details were not readily apparent," Holmes said to me as we sat in our rooms in Baker-street a few days later.

"Not to me," I confessed.

"At the time, I remarked on the significance of those bottles, did I not ? It was obvious that there was a group of men, almost certainly engaged in some clandestine activity, who met in order to exchange some kind of goods of such a value to make it worthwhile their doing so. You yourself suggested several items that might form the subject of such transactions. We rejected the romantic notions of pearls or other jewels, given their relative rarity in that area. Had the location being closer to London or some other major metropolis, I might have given more credence to that theory, but in a remote rustic area it was somewhat inconceivable that this would be the case."

"I follow you so far," I replied. "So much is logical."

"We had already determined, had we not, that the items so exchanged would be small and valuable, ruling out the possibility of their being more conventional contraband. I confess that I was somewhat at a loss to determine the exact nature of these goods until I suddenly recollected Sir Roderick's skill in the field of chemistry. What, I then asked myself, could be the result of Sir Roderick's efforts in that field ? It did not take me long to determine that the answer was probably some kind of narcotic drug. The exact nature of such a drug, until we actually visited Sir Roderick, and you supplied me with the article in your medical journal dealing with the same, escaped me."

"You had already linked this mysterious nocturnal gathering with Sir Roderick, then ? " I asked him.

"I could see no other way in which Sir Roderick could be acquiring his income. I had already examined the relevant records of the Stock Exchange, and the Prime Minister had already given me authority to search through the records of his bankers, in which I discovered nothing untoward. It was obvious that any source of his wealth was being derived through cash transactions, rather than any financial manipulations on paper. This argued that the transactions were being carried out between him and a lower class of person, rather than between him and his peers. The combination of the expensive cigar end and the common beer bottles we discovered in the orchard also supported this theory."

"I do not follow your reasoning here, Holmes," I exclaimed. "You clearly remarked to me on that occasion that the smoker of that cigar was missing a prominent tooth, a right incisor if I recall correctly, and I clearly observed that Sir Roderick was in possession of all his teeth, at least those at the front of his mouth."

Holmes smiled at me. "Your memory is not at fault. Have you never heard of dentures ? "

"Of course," I replied, "but what reason could ever convince you that Sir Roderick's teeth were false ? "

"There were two points on that matter that were convincing. The first was Sir Roderick's refusal to sample the apple that I offered him when we visited his house."

"Ah, those apples," I remarked ruefully. "I remember them well."

"On its own, that would have told me nothing, but it provided additional circumstantial evidence that made me suspect Sir Roderick still further. Wearers of false teeth typically are not that desirous of biting into such fruit. The unfortunate accident to your own tooth, Watson, was actually of considerable value to me. While you were having your tooth attended to, I was in the fortunate position of being able to examine the dental records of the patients, unknown to the dentist, and, as I had suspected, Sir Roderick was among their number. From them I was able to confirm positively that Sir Roderick's right incisor was indeed a prosthesis. In addition, as you no doubt remarked for yourself, the chemical stains on the fingers of his right hand told me plainly that he had been engaging in chemical experiments. All circumstantial evidence only, as I am sure you are about to remark, but an additional nail in the coffin of his innocence."

"I begin to understand a little more. But what about the charade with the two Chinamen and the cormorant ? That seemed to me to display, if I may say so, more than a touch of the theatrical."

Holmes shrugged, as if in apology. "Maybe it was," he confessed. "However, it was the best I could devise on the spur of the moment. I had determined that Sir Roderick was using the lighthouse for his own purposes. That fact has since been confirmed, by the way, by Trinity House, whose authorities have interviewed the lighthouse keeper there and ascertained that for several years he had accepted money from Sir Roderick in return for the use of certain buildings there as laboratories for Sir Roderick's chemical work, including the manufacture of the 'Heroin', though he appears to be innocent of any other involvement in the business. He must, however, have had his suspicions about the nocturnal sailings of Sir Roderick's yacht, somewhat aptly named *Morpheus*."

"Sir Roderick's rent was presumably of sufficient magnitude as to ensure his silence, I take it ? "

"Most probably. I was almost convinced beyond all doubt of this, but required still more evidence with which to provide the Prime Minister, as well as to satisfy my own standards. My goal was to prove, at least to my own satisfaction, that Sir Roderick was engaged in some business at the lighthouse, a place, you will surely admit, where he had no business to be."

"Surely it would have been possible merely to make your own visit and confirm these matters for yourself ? "

"I would have had no right to enter the premises, and any attempt to force an entry could have rebounded with most unpleasant consequences to the Government if any publicity were to ensue. No, Watson, I had to use some sort of guile in order to establish this fact for myself."

"Such as producing a spectacle of such a nature that sheer curiosity would divert Sir Roderick from whatever he was doing at the time, in order to watch it ? "

"Indeed, Watson. Although such evidence is once again merely circumstantial, the importance of discovering Sir Roderick at the lighthouse dressed in a laboratory coat, in combination with the other clues I discovered, would be sufficiently damning to Sir Roderick's prospects. The appearance of the exotic Chinese fishermen, and their strange method of obtaining the fish from the sea would be, I was sure, of sufficient novelty to draw out not only the lighthouse keeper, but any other inhabitants of the buildings, including Sir Roderick, to observe this strange phenomenon."

I shook my head. " I can see why you did not wish to involve the police," I said, "since an open scandal was to be avoided, but it does seem to me that the use of a trained cormorant in order to flush out your quarry was somewhat excessive in its quaintness."

Holmes chuckled in reply. "You may well be right there. But the results have been highly satisfactory, it must be admitted. As to the events on the final night, I have to confess I was somewhat mistaken in my first assumption of the events that were to transpire."

"I was expecting Sir Roderick to be distributing the 'Heroin' to his crew, and yet we saw none, did we not ? "

"I, too, was expecting the same, and it puzzled me briefly. When Sir Roderick brazenly invited me to search his boat, and I looked into his eyes, it was clear that there was no point in my doing so – there would be nothing to be found."

"What, then ? "

"For reasons best known to Sir Roderick, and the chain of malefactors responsible for the distribution of this foul substance, my surmise, which I have no doubt has been confirmed by Sir Roderick in his interview with the Prime Minister, is that the drug was distributed on the first night to the boatmen, who then received payment for it from those who push the substance into the market, as it were, and then bring the money to Sir Roderick on the following night, presumably retaining some portion of it as payment for their services."

" I can conceive of no other explanation at present."

" Nor I. It would seem to expose Sir Roderick and his confederates to considerable risk of detection, given that they will be busy on two successive nights, but as I remarked earlier, there are no doubt reasons that are unknown to us at present, and quite possibly likely to remain so, as to why Sir Roderick selected this method of operation."

" What will be the future developments in this case ? " I asked.

" As a result of the report that I presented personally to the Prime Minister yesterday evening, we can expect to seethe resignation of Sir Roderick Gilbert-Pryor announced in the press either this evening or tomorrow morning. The Prime Minister was instantly convinced of the urgency of the situation and arranged a meeting with Sir Roderick immediately I left Downing-street. Given the delicate state of relations that currently pertains between this kingdom and the Austro-Hungarian Empire, this is without doubt the wisest course of action, as it is essential that Sir Roderick's successor be appointed as soon as possible."

" It seems you have done a great service to the nation," I replied. " Are you not concerned, though, that Sir Roderick will seek some kind of revenge upon you for the harm you have done to his reputation ? "

" I am certain that such will be the case. He has made the acquaintance of one of the confederates of the late Professor James Moriarty, a certain Dr. Juliusz Sommerfeld of the University of Krakow. It is to be feared that the union of two such extraordinarily talented and yet perverted minds may make it inconvenient to stay in London for the next month or so. I therefore propose that we take a true vacation this time, somewhere far from the attentions that are likely to be visited on me by these true gentlemen. Have you anywhere in mind ? You mentioned Deauville, I seem to recall."

"I must confess, Holmes, that I have long desired to see the Great Pyramids of the Pharaohs in Egypt."

"And why should we not do so ? " enquired Holmes in reply.

"The expense, Holmes, the expense," I objected.

He smiled at me. "The Prime Minister was kind enough to offer me some compensation in return for the small service that I rendered to him. Naturally, I declined the honour of appearing as Sir Sherlock Holmes, but he was kind enough to fall in with my suggestion that I be allowed to retain the proceeds of Sir Roderick's enterprises that we collected the other evening. I am happy to say that the amount is quite considerable, and will be sufficient for us to travel to Egypt in the kind of style to which you and I are unfortunately little accustomed. It will make for a pleasant change of air, and I look forward with pleasure to continuing my research on the hidden meanings of some of the hieroglyphic symbols in the temples there that have so far eluded scholars."

The singular nature of this story, where Dr. Watson has in this instance failed to protect the identity of the major protagonist by a pseudonym, would seem to indicate that Holmes and Watson indeed feared an attack by Sir Roderick Gilbert-Foyle, possibly with the assistance alluded to by Holmes, and were reserving this account for possible publication in the event of such an outrage. This, of course, is borne out by Dr. Watson's original statement quoted at the beginning of this story, and is given

further support by the following written in a different hand on the final page.

"I, Sherlock Holmes, do hereby declare and attest that the account above written by John Watson MD, is a true and accurate description of my doings and associated events in the town of Falmouth, in the County of Cornwall, in July 1897. I hereby give my hand and seal," and then follows an almost illegible signature, of which the first word can be seen to commence with an S, and the second with an H. There is a witness, with the name printed as "Mrs. M Hudson", and the occupation given as "householder", and a signature in blue ink, in an obviously feminine hand, below Holmes' signature. The date is given as September 1897, from which we may conclude that Watson used some of his time in Egypt to pen this account of his and Holmes' adventure, making a fair copy on his return.

OTHER BOOKS BY HUGH ASHTON

CPSIA information can be obtained
at www.ICGtesting.com
Printed in the USA
LVHW012227130520
655436LV00005B/160